# SIMPLE HEART

Also by Cho Haejin

*I Met Loh Kiwan*

# SIMPLE HEART

CHO HAEJIN

TRANSLATED FROM THE KOREAN BY JAMIE CHANG

Other Press
*New York*

First published in Korean as 단순한 진심 (Dan-soon-han Jin-shim)
in 2019 by Minumsa Publishing Co., Ltd, Seoul



English-language translation rights arranged with
Minumsa Publishing Co., Ltd through New River Literary Ltd.

Production editor: Yvonne E. Cárdenas
Designed and typeset in Adobe Jenson Pro

1 3 5 7 9 10 8 6 4 2



Library of Congress Cataloging-in-Publication Data
Names: Cho, Hae-jin, 1976- author | Chang, Jamie translator
Title: Simple heart / Cho Haejin ; translated from the Korean
by Jamie Chang.
Other titles: Tansun han chinsim. English
Description: New York : Other Press, 2026.
Identifiers: LCCN 2025032773 (print) | LCCN 2025032774 (ebook) |
ISBN 9781635425819 paperback | ISBN 9781635425826 ebook
Subjects: LCGFT: Novels | Fiction
Classification: LCC PL994.17.H34 T3613 2026 (print) |
LCC PL994.17.H34 (ebook)
LC record available at https://lccn.loc.gov/2025032773
LC ebook record available at https://lccn.loc.gov/2025032774

# SIMPLE HEART

# I

I came from darkness.

Darkness trapped in the intangible frame of eternity, of stagnant time—that is my origin. Without direction, without knowing where I was to go, I drifted alone. What form did I take then—a hard, round seed; a tendril of smoke? Perhaps a mutable substance tumbling down or blowing away at the slightest reverberation, or even a formless pinch of energy.

In darkness I was formed and tearing the darkness apart I was born. I have no parents, or parents' parents, who related tales of prophetic dreams when I was in the womb or remembered the sound of my cry when I came into the world, or relatives or neighbors who photographed the moment when I first crawled, sat, stood, spoke. I don't have family records detailing the personal information of my parents, a birth certificate bearing my official date and time of birth, or medical records from the hospital where I was born, either. In their place are documents put together to ensure a smooth adoption process: an improvised single-person family record, adoption agreement signed by a stand-in guardian, international certificate of vaccination, travel permit, invoice for adoptive parents' coordinator to interpret and help the process along, receipt for the adoption agency fee (physical disabilities qualified for a discount, so I must have cost the full fee as a non-disabled child). Perhaps these records are still kept somewhere in Korea at an adoption agency or a government organization that oversees adoption.

Had someone kept my umbilical cord? When the question arises, sometimes my hands find themselves gently feeling around my belly button. But my belly button is but a vestige of my birth mother, incapable of recreating a single fingertip of hers. Ineffectual evidence, symbol without distinction, closed passageway . . . Her looks and impressions, scent and touch, tone and voice, her expression when she laughs or cries, her sleeping habits and complexes—I do not know these things, and it will be impossible to obtain such information in the future as well.

She, too, is a darkness to me.

—

Last June, I thought of her for the first time in a long while.

I was lying on an exam table at a small obstetrician's clinic in downtown Paris, looking up at the tiny movement on the ultrasound screen until my eyes hurt. Parts joined together that were presumed to be head, torso, and limbs wiggled on the screen. The silver-haired doctor, who introduced herself as Docteur Joubet, offered a word of congratulations and told me that it had been nine weeks since this new life came to me.

Joubet said, "Did you know a fertilized egg goes through tens of billions of years of evolutionary process in roughly 280 days? The single-cell fertilized egg divides continually as it becomes an amphibian, reptile, mammal, and the most physiologically complex mammal, the human. You're at nine weeks, so three weeks from now all the organs, including the genitals, will be fully formed. This is when the clay is molded, so to speak. You must be careful."

That was the moment my birth mother came to mind. I thought of her even though I had no memory of her, and this thought led to a yearning to see her. The shape of this yearning was unexpectedly large, round, and elaborate. It was a little bit baffling because in the past I had been curious about her and even wanted to find her, but never with this sense of yearning.

I left the clinic but instead of heading home I took a walk along a nearby footpath. A row of tall trees stood along the path, leaves intricately connecting to form a green canopy as

I thought about the life I held within me. I placed two possible options on either side of an imaginary scale and tried to measure them as accurately as I could. Sunlight filtered through the canopy of leaves overhead, casting a radial pattern of light. I stopped and threw my head back to gaze up at the undulating leaves. The trees stretched up toward the sky, and beyond the sky was the universe.

Universe.

*Wooju.*

I said "universe" to myself once again in Korean. The disquiet leading up to the moment dissipated, leaving only the name Wooju. It would not be difficult for the French to pronounce, and the universe, which held everything in existence, was the farthest thing from an indeterminate darkness. There was no need for deliberation. Or rather, I was done deliberating. This little life inside me—its fragile, freshly formed heart circulating blood through its body to increase the production of cells and undertaking the evolutionary process at miraculous speed—was given the name Wooju. I thought, *I must remember this moment.* Which way the wind was blowing, what color the leaves were, what the clouds looked like before they scattered—I will remember and tell Wooju when the child obtains language. From now on, I must remember every moment. I am the intermediary between Wooju and the world, the harbinger of their existence to the people of this world, and witness-bound to testify to their process of growing up. I will never neglect these roles and I will never let Wooju contemplate such things as darkness.

Under the trees on the footpath that day, this vow became the sole certainty of my life.

The day I found out that Wooju had come to me, I received another email from a Korean woman called Seoyeong.

When I returned to my place that evening, I sank back on the couch and opened my email like always. Seoyeong's name immediately caught my eye. She had first emailed me a week before, introducing herself as a woman of twenty-nine who had made several independent films since college, where she had studied film. She had an idea for a documentary with me—French adoptee from Korea, theater actor, playwright—as the main character.

She had written:

*I came across your interview one year ago. It was around that time I happened to hear that the old woman who runs a restaurant on the ground floor of my building once fostered a child soon to be adopted overseas. The experience opened my eyes to the fact that all my life I'd been ignorant of adoption or that adoptees existed. That might have been why I couldn't stop thinking about you,*

*Nana. I kept thinking and thinking, and a script about you formed in my head.*

*This is what I have in mind so far: visiting the places you passed through in Korea before you were adopted in France; looking for the people you came across; and finding out the meaning of your former name, Munju. As you know, Korean names have their own meaning, which is hard to infer just by the lettering or pronunciation. Nana, if it's not too forward of me, I'd like to ask what you think of working on this film with me in Korea.*

At the time I thought that the offer was in no way realizable. Putting my life in Paris on hold and going to Korea to be in a film by an amateur director whose work wasn't vouched for was as foolish as playing a game in which the only outcome is guaranteed defeat. It made me laugh. Still, I kept thinking about the email. A few days later, I sent a one-line reply asking why the interest in the name of an adoptee like me. This second email was probably the answer to that question.

The interview Seoyeong mentioned had taken place a year before, when I visited Korea for the first time in thirty-four years to attend an NGO program for overseas adoptees. I had heard that the main purpose of the program was to help adoptees find their birth families and organize reunions.

I suppose the interview request came to me because out of the fifteen adoptees I was the only one who hadn't found my family by the time the two-week program approached the halfway point. Besides, my Korean was fluent compared to that of the other adoptees. I had always been exposed to the language even after I left, so I was able to speak, listen, read, and write without much struggle. When I was young, Henri and Lisa bought me Korean storybooks and animated films, and as I grew older I watched Korean TV dramas and films I found on my own. I also did a language exchange in college with Kihyun, a Korean architecture student, for nearly four years. Kihyun had advised that I had to know hanja to master advanced Korean, so I taught myself the Chinese characters commonly used in Korean with a textbook I picked up at a used bookstore.

The interview had taken place on the second Tuesday of August on the second floor of a café in Gwanghwamun, Seoul. I was as forthcoming as I could be in describing the circumstances before and surrounding my adoption. The railroad tracks. The train conductor who saved me. What he looked like and my guess at his age. The atmosphere in the train conductor's house where I lived for a year and went by the name Munju. The name of the orphanage I was sent to after. And finally, I pulled out the passport I had kept with me since I boarded the plane to France thirty-four years before and opened it to the photo page. The passport was a rush job done right before my adoption, and I had brought it to offer all the clues I had to someone out there who might remember me. The journalist, who was typing away on her laptop, looked up and smiled at me.

"I'm sure you have more stories to tell . . . What's your life in France like?" she asked. "You've returned to your homeland after a long time. I'd love to know what your experience in Seoul has been like too."

I gazed at the journalist. While she couldn't have known that I had pinned every last bit of hope I had on this interview, in that moment I felt an uncontrollable swell of disappointment wash over me. Disappointment, or maybe something closer to antagonism.

After the interview, the journalist left for another engagement.

As the sun went down and night grew deep, I sat motionless at the café, looking out the window. The rows of tents in Gwanghwamun Square sank into darkness. I knew from French news reports whom the tents were erected for us to never forget. It rained on the evening I saw the breaking news that the Sewol ferry had sunk, resulting in the deaths of 304 people, 250 of whom were high school students. Even a long, hot shower couldn't warm the chills in my body. My loneliness grew as I recalled that evening. I pictured a shipwreck survivor lost at sea with no one sent to find her—this person began to act out my loneliness. It was an old habit of mine, turning a real-life situation into a theatrical scene, conjuring an actor from my imagination, and projecting my loneliness onto her. This projection was of my loneliness but at the same time it was not mine alone, and in this way its depths were not too daunting.

I read the interview just once. The article was published in a magazine just before I left Korea, so I was able to receive it by post. As I'd predicted, the three-page article was more about my life now than my life before I was adopted. A French cultural foundation playwriting award that I had received not long before was played up quite a bit. The passport photo I had asked them to run didn't make it into the spread. Based on the photograph taken at the café in Gwanghwamun, it was impossible to tell that I had once been a child who was abandoned on the train tracks or that I had gone by the name Munju. I had staked every last bit of hope in me that the person who had named me Munju and my birth mother would read the story and reach out, but I never heard from either of them.

I gazed at the computer screen for a good long while, then checked the box next to Seoyeong's email and hit delete. I didn't know Seoyeong, and I didn't know anything about the hours she'd spent thinking about Munju. The hours between the moment she happened to read about me in a magazine, let her imagination rise, and sketch out a documentary—the shape, texture, and substance of those hours were in a realm unknown to me.

I tried to close the laptop, but my hand did not comply. *Don't be so dramatic,* I said to myself. I could always delete Seoyeong's email after reading her response to my question. I logged back in, recovered the email I'd just deleted, and slowly read the contents.

If I hadn't recovered Seoyeong's email, if I hadn't participated in her documentary, I would have gone about my life without ever having known the people I met in Korea, and that life would have been like a book with the most important pages missing. Empty . . . unimaginably so. Whatever I am in the present, I could never return to who I was before I knew them.

*Because a name is a house,* Seoyeong's second email began.

*I think our names are a kind of house where our identity or sense of self reside. People forget everything so quickly here. I truly believe that remembering a name is how we pay our respects to the forgotten worlds.*

Identity. Sense of self. House. Respect. Seoyeong's choice of words caught my attention. "Caught my attention" does not nearly describe their effect. I had yearned for these words more ardently than anything in life. Before long, I was sitting straight up on my sofa, concentrating on Seoyeong's email.

It appeared Seoyeong's project was already well underway. The synopsis and even the sequence were already set, the staff assembled and the agreement signed with her university, which had a strong film program that rented relatively new camera and lens models. She couldn't cover my travel expenses or pay me well, but she'd attached photos of the free accommodation I would have over the two to three months of shooting. I clicked on the image files. Pictures of a small living room, bedroom, and the view from the window popped up, one after the other.

*This is the place I rent. It's not fancy, as you can see, but it'll be comfortable for one person. Besides, you get a view of Namsan Tower lit up at night,* Seoyeong said.

As I looked through the photos, hazy memories of the train conductor's house, which had been sort of a foster home for me, emerged. A weathered hanok at the end of an alley. When it rained, the smell of wood seeped into every corner of the house, suffusing the air with a spicy, mint-like scent. A rainy day also meant getting to eat a brownish-purple dumpling-shaped treat. The train conductor's mother would click her tongue disapprovingly at me every time our eyes met, but when we were sitting under the awning and sharing the treat to the sound of rain, she was as affectionate as if she were my real grandmother. Ground sweet red bean was spooned into the pocket of dough, fried in oil, and sprinkled with sugar. I couldn't remember the name of that dish, and once I left Korea I never saw it again. But the taste of it had been lingering on the tip of my tongue for a few days. I believed a bite of that treat, which I couldn't possibly find in France, would instantly cure the nausea that plagued me at all hours of the day. I was of course aware that flying long-distance at the beginning of a pregnancy just to satisfy a craving was not a rational decision, and that I had to be careful like the doctor said.

At that point, I should have deleted Seoyeong's email or sent a standard rejection letter. But I did not. Instead, I remembered something I'd read in a brochure on Korea: *Many pregnant women return to their parents' home for a while to eat well and prepare for the delivery*—and prepared myself to be swayed. But more than anything, the possibility of finding the train conductor or his mother, however remote, overwhelmed all the unfavorable aspects of the journey. It contained hope—that if I could find out the meaning of "Munju" and shed just a little more light on my origins, I'd be able to welcome Wooju into the world with more confidence.

It was the train conductor who saved me on the railroad tracks.

More precisely, he pulled the emergency brake and saved me from being run over. For whatever reason, he didn't take the scared, crying girl of unknown origin to the police station or orphanage; instead, he took her home, where he lived with his mother, gave her the name Munju, and protected her. If a name is a house, like Seoyeong said, I lived in that name for nearly a year. "Munju" was never recorded in any documents or registered in official systems. It was only used by the train conductor, his mother, and some of their neighbors, and disappeared when I was sent to the orphanage. I didn't know why my temporary protector and the person to whom I owed my life gave me the name Munju, but it was clear that it came from a place of kindness. What else could it have been? He was the only adult who patted me on the head at meals and told me to eat lots and lots. He often brought home handmade biscuits for me, and on days when his mother nagged him to "hurry up and do something about that wretched girl," he'd pick me up, swing me around on his back, and take me for a walk.

For a long time, I couldn't even try to look for him. The sugary taste of the biscuits, the soft palms of his hands, the feel of the hard bones on his back, and the sound of his baritone voice reverberating in the helix of my ear, pressed against him as he called "Munju"—one couldn't find a person with just a few sensory memories. According to the rough estimate of the doctor at the clinic, based on my development I was only three or four years old then, not old enough to have written down his name or address for a future reunion.

The kindly staff of the NGO that invited me to Korea one year ago were as amiable to the adoptees as they could be, but they couldn't help me. To find a person who was not family, without his name, age, or social registration number, was beyond their capacity. Unable to find him, I couldn't find out the meaning of the name Munju.

*Door pillars.*

I had once depended on door pillars as a consolation. Kihyun, my language exchange partner in college, found the word in the Korean dictionary, and I had made up my mind to go with that definition. I had buried my face in Kihyun's dictionary, reading the definition over and over again: *munju,* n.: *Pillars erected on either side of a frame to install a door.* Truth be told, I was overjoyed that day. I knew that people seldom chose a word that appeared in the dictionary as a name, but I liked that "munju" was familiar to Koreans and that the image of "door pillars" was as foreign as it was entrancing. Pillars rooted in the ground to support the roof and at the same time serve as the center of a building's gravity, door pillars were artifacts of a faraway land to me.

*Munju, door pillars.* Saying the words one after the other brought comfort.

But my untenable assumption of the meaning of munju would not last as a source of comfort. The more I depended on it, the more my door pillars wobbled, then crumbled a little at a time, eventually turning indistinct and intangible.

Having learned the lesson that faith in unreliable information can be even more disappointing than not knowing, I lost the habit of incanting *munju, door pillars* whenever I was in agony or turmoil. The comforting effect did not last.

Friends asked why I was so obsessed with a temporary name from the past. I had just one answer for them: Munju was my origin. Before I was called Munju, before I was found on the railroad tracks, my life was but a stretch of darkness from which I could retrieve no memories. Not being able to remember anything before the age of three or four could be considered normal depending on an individual's development; but for me the lack of memories could have been a result of the shock I experienced from the railroad track incident, as a psychotherapist I saw in college had suggested. Because there was no memory from before; my name before I was found—though my birth mother may not have bothered with the small task of naming me—had passed into oblivion as well. I was able to retain senses and memories from the time when my life as Munju began. A whole being who can tell sweet from bitter, say what she likes and doesn't like, feel bored, wronged, sorry. All the memories of my firsts—the first word I said out loud, the inside of the first restaurant and hair salon I went to, what made me laugh or cry for the first time, and the first moment I knew what it was to be abandoned—they all belonged to Munju. For my history to begin, I had to know the meaning of Munju.

This was what I had said during the interview one year ago.

*If the meaning of "Munju" isn't discovered, that failure will be the conclusion of the film.*

Seoyeong's email ended with this sentence. It was strange. In the message delivered in the default font of the email program she was using, I heard an unworried voice that seemed to say it was okay to be reckless for once in my life. In that moment, my swaying heart became still. This time, I wouldn't worry about being disappointed again; I would just think of this journey as a few months' vacation eating the dumpling-shaped food the train conductor's mother had made for me and resting up for the baby.

Seoyeong's invitation was perhaps a stroke of good luck.

I wrote back to her and accepted the invitation.

The very next day, I began to prepare for the trip. I went back to Docteur Joubet and received confirmation that it was safe to fly long-distance after twelve weeks, and if possible I should return before twenty-seven weeks to prepare for delivery. I got international health insurance, renewed my travel visa, and sublet my studio apartment to an actor friend. On the day I notified the chief director of the theater company I belonged to that I wanted to take a yearlong sabbatical, I called Lisa from the tram home.

Five years ago, Lisa had moved to Montpellier, a town on the Mediterranean in the south of France, where she lived alone. Montpellier had been Henri's hometown. I only told Lisa that I would be traveling to Korea, not that she would soon become Wooju's grandmother. Since Henri's death, we'd grown apart, and sharing something so personal felt awkward. We weren't particularly close when Henri was alive, but his absence brought a new dimension to our relationship: the unspoken feeling that surviving family members should look out for each other and share the burden of their troubles, and our guilt for failing to do that.

Besides, I knew what was missing in Lisa. If Wooju's existence triggered the slightest possibility of reminding Lisa of what she lacked, I wouldn't be able to bear it. *I trust you,* Lisa said on the other end of the line. Lisa always said that. Declarations like *I worry about you, I love you, my daughter* weren't Lisa's style. We discussed how summer was rapidly approaching in Montpellier, an upcoming Godard retrospective that would be showing in a few theaters, then wrapped up the call with laughter.

A month later, I boarded a plane to Korea with Wooju at fourteen weeks, armed with the excuse that I was going to find the meaning of Munju. But buried deep inside was the selfish thought that I didn't really care what happened with the film.

It was an unexpected homecoming, just one year later.

# 2

*Unexpected homecoming.* There were no other words for it.

Upon my return to France a year ago, after the ten-day program with Korean adoptees from all over the world, I had vowed never to go back to Korea again. While other adoptees had used their photographs, documents, letters, and other clues to reunite with their birth parents and siblings, I'd stayed back at the hotel watching TV or drinking beer. But that wasn't the only reason I stayed in my room. I was suffering from a loneliness more palpable than I had ever experienced before, of a kind that nearly crippled me.

In France, I had believed that something in me would finally be compensated if I could just go to Korea. Henri and Lisa were wonderful parents and I fully acknowledged that I was lucky to be matched with a very compatible family, but my identity was like a tree that had been uprooted and replanted in a place where it couldn't help but draw attention. For instance, as a child I had never thrown tantrums or demanded things like expensive school supplies, a road trip, or a big, raucous birthday party. When I had a stomach ache or a fever, I lay quietly in bed pretending to be asleep, and when boys at school harassed me with their racist, sexual comments, I did not tell Henri and Lisa. When we went out to eat, I studied the menu for items that were cheaper than Henri and Lisa's choices, and obeyed every rule at school so they wouldn't have to deal with the nuisance of being called in. The compensation I was looking for was not extravagant. Being true to my feelings from moment to moment, expressing my dislikes and complaints without fear of offending, asking without hiding the hurt why they'd abandoned me, why they didn't come looking for me—if I ever met my birth mother or the train conductor, these were the things I wanted to do. That was all.

But that was a delusion.

Served me right to get my hopes up despite having scant to no information about my birth mother and the train conductor. As I came to terms with the fact that they were far beyond reach, I sank deeper into loneliness. And when I hit the bottom, I found helplessness. So I didn't sightsee or shop, nor did I participate in communal cooking classes and other socializing events. When the NGO staff made a special effort to include me, I recoiled from their friendliness and concern. I got the sense that they were taking pity on me in the typical way Koreans pitied Korean adoptees, and reading into their every nice gesture would have exhausted a lifetime's worth of energy.

Toward the end of the two-week program, I spent nearly all day holed up in the suite, the only pleasant part of the day being my midnight walk around the neighborhood watching the lights go out one by one. I liked the moment when Seoul, city of light, went dark like a store closing for the day. Or rather, what I waited to see wasn't my surroundings falling into complete darkness, but the traffic lights, the twenty-four-hour convenience stores and restaurants emitting light that never went out. Buildings that always had one or two windows lit up no matter how deep the night looked, like enormous, luminescent creatures hidden under dark, holey tarps. The multi-vision billboards at the top of the buildings beamed beautiful mute women. The silent fluorescent thrumming spoke to me, and I snuck out and wandered every night at midnight just to hear it.

I didn't manage to find anyone through the program, but I did meet two adoptees I would remember for a long time.

One was my roommate, Suzy from Denmark. One night

after my midnight walk, I returned to the suite to find Suzy's bed empty but the sound of running water coming from the bathroom. I went into the bathroom, assuming Suzy had stepped out for a moment and forgotten to turn off the tap, but there she was sitting in the half-filled tub in the same outfit she'd been wearing earlier that day. Suzy had just turned twenty-five and was the youngest among the fifteen adoptees.

She had found her birth family easily, and had gone out nearly every day to see her birth mother and sisters. When I asked her what was wrong, she slowly looked up, her lips blue from the cold water. I turned off the tap and handed Suzy a towel and bathrobe. Moments later, she came out of the bathroom in the robe, and I helped her to the bed, carefully laying her down. She rolled over to face the wall and said that being with her family did not make her happy, that she was only pretending, that everything seemed fake.

"I'm eating or shopping with them, and suddenly I feel myself leaving my body, coldly watching myself play a part in a skit called 'Reunited Family.' It's always like that when I'm with them. They're not the family I'd been dreaming of. Honestly, I thought they would be tragically poor. But it turns out they have a house and a car. Both my sisters went to college. Mom even has an old dog. So shameless. I never asked to be born, and yet they brought me into the world and then sent me to a faraway country without my permission or consent. But they have a *dog*. They have no idea that a dozen times a day I picture myself stabbing them all with a knife, crushing them under my foot, and tossing their bodies out to rot."

Suzy cried herself to sleep that night. I sat beside her, rubbing her back when it shook. It was nearly dawn when she finally managed to fall asleep. Curled up in a tight ball like a child, frowning as if she were in a bad dream, Suzy slept as I watched over her.

Steve from the US was the other adoptee. Adopted in the late 1970s, Steve was about ten years older than me and couldn't speak Korean at all, except for a few greetings. He was short but broad-shouldered with a keen look in his eyes that made him remind me of a retired boxer, but he was actually a chef. At the farewell party held at a nearby bar on the last night of the program, Steve and I sat next to each other at the far end of the table. He and I were the only adoptees who weren't reunited with our families—Steve because he refused to meet them. As the others chatted over the loud music about the trips they'd taken with their families, Steve and I silently emptied our drinks. The party was winding down when Steve asked me if my birth mother or father was overseas. Esme, an American adoptee around my age who was sitting in the center seat, was saying especially loudly that adoption was the greatest opportunity of her life. *No,* I answered him with a faint smile. *Are they in prison? No. Are they dead? I haven't checked and I honestly don't know anything about them.* As Steve and I fell silent again, Esme claimed loudly that she wouldn't have become a lawyer if her birth mother hadn't put her up for adoption, and a chorus of voices protested or concurred.

When the noise died down, Steve said: "I was adopted to the Minnesota countryside when I was seven. I traveled twenty hours to get there and found out I had three stepbrothers. All adopted. All different nationalities and races. Turns out, my adoptive parents kept buying kids for free labor at the corn farm and the tax benefits. Literal fucking shit. As soon as I turned eighteen, I was out of there. I went to the city and cleaned buildings, worked down at the docks, anything I could find. I missed Umma but I couldn't find her without her ID number or address. Besides, I didn't have the financial means. Time passed, and I reached this age. I'd pretty much given up, but my kid was born last year. Seeing him revived my will to look for her. That's how I signed up for this program. I actually did figure out her whereabouts on this trip. She's in a southern province rotting away in a homeless shelter. Fucking hell. What's worse is that she's got this mental illness that erased her memory of the son she once had. Took me forty years to find Umma, and I didn't go see her. I think the person I was looking for wasn't a biological mother but a mother in the emotional sense, who would apologize to me. Or maybe even something more than that. A mother who is ashamed that she abandoned her son, who begs for forgiveness in tears. Umma's going to die soon. I'm the only child she ever had and she has no parents or husband, so she'll probably die alone. So I'll have no one left to forgive, forever."

Steve knocked back the rest of his beer and added quietly, with his eyes fixed on the glass, "You're lucky."

# 3

Nine in the morning Korea time, I got through customs and came out of the double doors. I saw two people holding up a sign that read "Munju." I made my way toward them, dragging a suitcase in each hand, and the woman with the camera bag on her shoulder gave me a brief hug. It was Seoyeong.

Accompanying Seoyeong was a woman who majored in film at the same art college. I was told she had graduated earlier that year and was now applying to grad school programs. With her bob, boyish outfit, and small frame, she looked more like an adolescent boy than a grown woman. Perhaps more so next to Seoyeong, who was wearing a form-fitting dress and had long wavy hair. Her name was Soyul. When I asked them what their names meant by the benches at the arrival gate, they smiled and told me. Seoyeong was *seo* as in "dawn" and *yeong* as in "crystal." Crystal dawn. Soyul was *so* as in "little" and *yul* as in "chestnut tree." Little chestnut tree. *Crystal dawn, little chestnut tree,* I said to myself several times as if determined not to forget, and then recorded it in my phone notepad.

Seoyeong said in an animated tone, like someone who'd just remembered something very important, that she and Soyul had completed five short films together during their college years. She said with a proud look on her face that their latest film, which they'd completed last year, was funded by the government and invited to screen at domestic film festivals. But unfortunately, she said sadly, none of their films had been officially released in theaters or made a profit.

"So money is always an issue," Seoyeong said with a bashful smile.

Because money was always an issue, they were never able to have an art department or computer graphics, or use music with existing copyright. Actors and staff had to be kept to a minimum as well, Seoyeong added. The working conditions for this documentary would be more or less the same, so I would be the only recurring character and Seoyeong would have a staff of three—including herself—the third staff member being Seoyeong's boyfriend, another fellow film major who had just belatedly completed his military service. Seoyeong laughed and said not to be too surprised when he showed up in old sweats when filming began. I could tell that Seoyeong was watching for my reaction. She was worried I'd be disappointed by the pitiful working conditions.

I wasn't disappointed in the least. On the contrary, it all felt familiar. Henri had always made films under such adverse conditions. Seoyeong and Soyul couldn't hide their astonishment when I told them that my adoptive father was a film director, and wanted to know about his works. I knew they weren't just being polite when they asked me to show them one of his films when I had the chance, but I couldn't give them a clear yes right away. I wasn't ready for the three of us to watch Henri's films over food and beer. If they didn't understand or like his work, I would most certainly be disappointed and would hold on to that disappointment for a long time.

Seoyeong changed the subject. "By the way, you said door pillars, right?"

I nodded, wondering if she was confirming what I'd said in the interview one year ago. Seoyeong pulled something up on her phone and handed it to me. It was the dictionary entry for munju.

"I looked it up, and *munju* also means 'dust' in a dialect in the northeastern region."

I stared at Seoyeong's phone. My surroundings darkened and the noise in the airport faded as if I were slowly being sucked into a long tunnel. Seoyeong must have planned to include this scene in the film; out of the corner of my eye, I could see her hurrying to turn the camera on and start filming. The red light on the camera bothered me, but the feeling soon dulled. All I could see was one word: *dust.*

Dust.

On the airport express heading to Seoul, I was still thinking about dust. Seoyeong was sitting to my right, carefully going over the footage from the airport, and Soyul was to my left, quietly nodding off.

A small, useless substance. Particles that must be removed for cleanliness. The final form all living things take before their hollow existence comes to a close. The more I thought about the definition, the greater my suspicions grew that "dust" was the real meaning of Munju. Because I had never settled in one place, blowing around in even the faintest breeze all my life. There were days when I pictured myself as a speck of dust traveling all over the world, and every time I thought *What if I had never been born?* an overwhelming feeling of betrayal washed over me and I wondered if the train conductor, contrary to the sensory memories ingrained in me, was a cruel man inside. *Fitting for a child abandoned on the railroad tracks to disappear without a single trace,* he may have thought. Was Munju a name that came from contempt and derision, instead of kindness? I looked out the window across the aisle. The vibrant summer landscape between Incheon and Seoul was unfurling outside, but it looked to me like a city on the verge of collapse under a thick layer of toxic dust.

"It's quite hot, huh?"

Soyul offered me a handkerchief. It must have been obvious that I was breaking out in a cold sweat. Looking down at the neatly folded checkered handkerchief, I felt the urge to tell her everything. *I'm with child. At the moment, the biggest part of me isn't dust but the universe—Wooju. Truthfully, I'm scared that my lack of maturity will harm Wooju. So could you promise to do me just one favor when I need it most?*

I couldn't.

We'd just met, and the women were more than ten years younger than I was. I didn't want to lean on them, nor did I have any reason to. They were taking on enough as it was to make a good film, and there was no reason to add my circumstances and health to their burden. After the shooting, I would leave Seoyeong's place and return to France before the twenty-seven-week mark, as the doctor advised, and prepare for the delivery. My belly would grow big, my body would change, and if my mood shifted from moment to moment in unexpected ways, I would deal with it alone, as I always had. And I had to be alone.

—

We got off at Noksapyeong Station. Seoyeong and Soyul each took one of my bags; they could see I was tired from the journey. When we got out of the station, we were greeted by the tall walls of a US Army base on one side and a procession of lush plane trees on the other. Seoyeong's apartment was in a neighborhood between Noksapyeong and Itaewon, a popular commercial district, and accessible by the local shuttle. Since it was my first day, we would walk to her place to help familiarize me with the neighborhood, but Seoyeong said it was best to use the local shuttle bus because the road was quite steep.

The uphill climb began. It was indeed steep, just as Seoyeong had warned, and cluttered with old houses lining both sides of the road. Interestingly, we came across many restaurants, bars, and coffee shops with stylish interiors in what appeared to be an ordinary residential area. The doors were flung open on all these establishments where people, most of them young women, drank and talked, read or worked on their laptops. It was a mishmash of past and present, decline and youth, residential and commercial. Seoyeong said that she had settled here when she first came to Seoul for college because the area was quite cheap. But ten years later the neighborhood unexpectedly became a hotspot. She would have to move when her lease was up because she couldn't afford the rent.

"Who's this development for?" Seoyeong suddenly cried dramatically.

We stopped walking, and I asked Soyul what this neighborhood was called.

"It's Itaewon. Yongsan-gu, Itaewon-dong. But the area where Seoyeong lives is more commonly called Haebangchon, but that's not its official name. It's a sort of nickname that it got when Korea gained independence from Japan, and the people who returned from overseas or came down from the north settled here."

"Do 'Yongsan' and 'Itaewon' mean anything?"

"Well . . ." Soyul must have never thought about what they meant. She scratched her head, looked something up on her phone, and after a while said, "Yongsan is named for the shape of the area, which looks like a dragon. *Yong*, 'dragon.' *San*, 'hill.'"

"And Itaewon? What does 'Itaewon' mean?" Seoyeong asked.

"There are apparently two origins for 'Itaewon,'" Soyul said. "There was a yeokwon here called Itae-won and the name remains today. 'Itae' comes from the large pear orchard that used to be here. The other origin is from the Joseon dynasty. After each war, violated women came to this area to give birth and settle down. People called them *itain*—'the different,' 'the other.' Some say that Itaewon comes from that term."

"The second sounds more likely," Seoyeong said. "There's a US Army base in Itaewon, lots of foreigners and exiled people, gay bars and Middle Eastern restaurants."

I quietly listened to Seoyeong and Soyul's conversation as we started up the hill again. Soyul, who had fallen behind a little, quickly caught up with me. She told me in a hushed voice, as if she were divulging a secret, that Joseon was the name of a premodern Korean dynasty and that *yeokwon* was a place where people traveling on horseback could rest for the night. I forced a smile for her. Words like *Joseon* and *yeokwon* meant as little to me as the name of an element on the periodic table or a planet with tricky spelling. The definition for *itain*—that was the only thing that stuck with me.

Twenty minutes later, we reached our destination. Seoyeong's building seemed rundown, but it was located at the top of the hill and had an unobstructed view of the street that had led us there. It was a great view.

On the ground floor of the three-story redbrick building was a restaurant. I stood in front of the restaurant and gazed up at the store sign that read, in green script against a white background, "Bokhee's Kitchen." The metal sign had likely never been fixed or washed since the day it was hung up, the letters faded and the four corners dinged. Without lighting installed, the sign could not fulfill its most basic function after sundown. I took a glance inside. There were no customers, and the old woman who appeared to be the owner was sitting at a table looking up at an old-fashioned box TV.

The moment I spotted her, I couldn't look away. This was the old woman Seoyeong had mentioned in her email, the one who had once looked after a child who was about to be adopted. At the airport, Seoyeong had said that she had found out about the old woman's history when someone from a children's welfare agency asked for directions to the restaurant. When Seoyeong brought it up with the old woman, which was around the time she came across my interview, the old woman suddenly turned cold and told her to mind her own business. Seoyeong stopped eating there.

The old woman was now sitting in her restaurant with her mouth hanging open, a drab floral-print apron over her T-shirt. A fly buzzed noisily around her, but she was as still as a statue. She was the very picture of old age I feared most. Loneliness turned to inertia and a cold rage aimed at the world were embodied in her stooped back and chalky complexion. I quickly turned away. I didn't want to picture my future self, cast aside by society, in another person. *Is Bokhee the old woman's name? Probably. Lonely, fat old woman in a store bearing her name,* I thought to myself as I tapped the heels of my sneakers on the ground.

To get to Seoyeong's third-floor apartment, one had to go through the wicket door in the iron gate and up the stairs along the outside wall of the building. The stairs were so narrow that Seoyeong, Soyul, and I had to climb the steps single file. There was a railing, but I reminded myself to be extra careful after dark. At fourteen weeks, Wooju's body was fully formed, but the bones were still soft and the blood thin. The organs would be delicate and the skin a thin mucous membrane. Wooju, a lump of clay that had not hardened yet, absolutely needed protection, and I was their only protector.

Twenty-seven steps led up to the third floor. One had to go through two doors to get into Seoyeong's unit, which meant memorizing two door codes. The main wicket door was for both units in the building, and the one further in on the right side led to Seoyeong's unit.

Seoyeong stood at an angle and slid open the keypad cover. I watched her closely as she entered the four-digit code.

The door opened to reveal a quaint space, like a fairy house. The open-concept studio apartment was divided into a living room and bedroom by a sliding door, Seoyeong explained. As soon as I took off my shoes, stepped inside, and put down my bags, Seoyeong led me around the unit by the hand. She took me to the kitchen, where she pointed out the pots and utensils, the spices, the coffee maker and toaster, then the bathroom, where she showed me how the washer and shower worked. Then she led me to the bedroom, which was on the other side of the sliding doors.

There was a mattress without a bedframe, a dark brown wardrobe, a bookcase and desk, a picture frame, a clock, and a few decorative pieces. I also noticed a sunny window behind blinds made of plain muslin, a halogen ceiling light, and a table lamp.

When we finished touring the apartment, I finally asked the one thing I had been dying to know: "So where will you sleep?"

This had been part of the deal: Seoyeong would accommodate me in her apartment free of charge for the two months or so it would take to shoot the film. Back in Paris, I had not thought about the fact that this would mean inconveniencing Seoyeong.

Seoyeong told me not to worry, that there were plenty of bath-and-sauna houses in Seoul where she could get a cheap place to sleep and she had many friends, including Soyul, who could put her up for the night, so one night per friend could cover as many as ten days. If she was truly out of options, she could stay with her boyfriend as a last resort. Her boyfriend still lived with his parents so she would have to sneak in and out, but she flashed a smile and said she had done it before.

From the kitchen, which was on the other side of the living room, came a smell that awakened my hunger. Seoyeong and I turned at the same time to see Soyul busy preparing toast, scrambled eggs, and coffee. Soyul must have cooked in this kitchen many times before, her movements swift and easy.

We had our late breakfast at the table in the living room. Seoyeong and Soyul got up as soon as we were done, saying I should rest for now, that the first shoot was in two days and I should sleep as much as I could to get over the jet lag. Before they left, Seoyeong handed me a piece of paper. It contained a map showing the supermarket, dry cleaner, and a restaurant where she was a regular. Above the map were the door codes in large handwriting.

It was an awful pain.

My sides and stomach were splitting and my inner thighs were burning. There was no one around. I lay alone on a metal bed in the dark. *Harder. More, more.* From the darkness came an androgynous voice that sounded like it was modulated by a machine. That voice was all I could rely on. I pushed and wrung several times from head to toe, so hard that the sinews in my neck and hands bulged, until I heard a baby cry and I felt emptied below. *Wooju,* I thought, and even though I was delirious with pain, a faint smile spread over my lips. A pair of pale hands emerged from the darkness and laid a bundled blanket next to me. With the back of my hand, I pushed a lock of hair clinging to my sweaty forehead, and gently reached inside the blanket.

The bundle was empty.

I sprang out of bed and shook the blanket out like a madwoman, but Wooju was not in there. The utter sense of loss turned to a coldness that froze my blood and my organs. My teeth chattered and my skin stung. I wasn't able to protect Wooju, and I was alone again—this was the reality I faced. Unable to take it anymore, I wailed, drawing up a long cry from deep inside. I cried and cried, mouth wide open, shoulders shaking violently, more destroyed than I had ever been.

When I managed to wake from the dream, I was still cold and shaking. I found the blanket bunched at my feet and covered myself up to my neck. I must have been asleep for a long time, as darkness was sitting in the room like a guest. By and by, it came to me that I was not in Paris, but Seoul—in my birth home, the home of my mother, but without a single person to comfort me after having woken from a bad dream. My hands found their way to my lower abdomen. In this moment of stupefying fear, the only real comfort was Wooju.

*Wooju.*

In the darkness, I gently called Wooju. And in that moment, I thought of her again, the woman I knew so little of; and what little I did know was based not on her, but on who I had become. I had come from her body forty-odd years ago and I had received her protection for at least three or four years. There was little else I could infer. She did not announce my existence to the world, and so perhaps she had kept my birth a secret. If so, she would have given birth at an unlicensed clinic that didn't require patient information. She wouldn't have had family, so she would have looked after me all by herself. That is to say, she handled the tedious labor that is childcare every single day for several years.

I pictured a woman with an affable, youthful face.

Isolated and confined to a small room with a baby she couldn't speak to, nursing her, feeding her mashed-up food, washing her with warm water, changing her, clipping her toenails and fingernails, burping her, and rubbing her belly until she fell asleep—these actions would not have been possible had she not been a kind, patient person. A woman who had not once thought of sinful acts, a woman with an air of purity who was in the habit of praying each time she held her baby—I preferred to picture her this way.

But not knowing what it was to sin, she could have committed a much greater evil because of her innocence. She gave birth to me and raised me, but she also left me on the train tracks. These train tracks represented sinful neglect and betrayed that she didn't care whether her daughter lived or died. A woman more frightful for her ignorance, a woman who left her crying baby alone in a room and went out at night, a woman who carelessly conceived many before and after me, who aborted many times and, failing that, abandoned a baby in any place, a woman anyone could buy with money, a woman who had never been treated with respect by another.

Once when I was in university, I visited the school counseling center. I had always wondered why I had sensory memories, if fragmented, of the time I lived as Munju, whereas memories of the time before that had passed into oblivion. That is, I wanted to know how the train tracks came to symbolize a dividing line between memory and oblivion. The counselor said that the earliest childhood memories adults retain are from when they were about three years old, and so if I was around three when I was discovered at the train tracks, it would be medically unremarkable if I didn't remember my birth mother. However, isolating a specific point in time, such as being found on the train tracks, and completely forgetting the rest suggested an involvement of my own will. It was the counselor's opinion that for a long time my subconscious wilfully blocked memories of my birth mother; it was almost as if I had sealed the memories in a black plastic sack, as it were.

"Of course, it's trauma. The train racing toward you on the train tracks would have left a psychological trauma. It's also possible that you were already traumatized when you were living with your birth mother. Perhaps you saw something you couldn't reconcile with, or perhaps you were abused."

The counselor didn't try to tiptoe around me or comfort me; instead, he gave me his blunt assessment for the sake of providing accurate information. At some point, I couldn't hear him anymore. I got up before the session was over and left without excusing myself. That was my first and last time in therapy.

I lay on the mattress for a long time before getting up. But when I flipped the light switch, the ceiling light didn't come on. I pulled back the curtain and looked outside to see that the nearby buildings were also dark. I used the light from my cell phone screen to search for a candle, but soon gave up. Seoyeong's place was small. In an apartment barely large enough to store the most basic necessities for eating, sleeping, washing, and discharge, it was doubtful she would have an in-case-of-emergency item such as a candle.

I gathered my keys, wallet, and the map Seoyeong had drawn for me. I was hungry since I had slept through lunch and dinner, and I couldn't stand the darkness any longer. But when I grabbed the door handle, I was seized by an unexpected fear that a pitch-black abyss would swallow me on the other side of the door. It was a familiar feeling. I had gone through the same thing thirty-five years ago, on my first night with Henri and Lisa. I had had a nightmare, and when I woke up, I'd pictured an abyss much like the one I was envisioning now and could not open the door even though I had urgently needed to go to the bathroom. *This will pass, it'll be nothing once it passes,* I reminded myself, taking a deep breath and slowly turning the door handle. When the door opened, there was no abyss, of course, just the stairwell. The steep road in the distance was bathed with light and the brightly lit Namsan Tower came into view. The power outage seemed to be an angel of indigence that touched only the houses at the top of the hill.

I groped around to find the railing and carefully made my way down the twenty-seven steps. I went out through the wicket door and was passing by Bokhee's Kitchen when a dim light flickering off the windowpane caught my eye. The restaurant was still empty. The old woman from that morning was sitting by candlelight, and the large, heaving shadow cast on the wall behind her was tenderly watching over her. Seoyeong had told me earlier in the day that Bokhee's Kitchen had opened around the time she'd moved into the building, but she had not once seen the place busy with customers. The restaurant didn't appear very sanitary, she said, and most of the dishes had too much salt, but Seoyeong surmised it was the old woman's aloofness that was unsuited to running a restaurant. In fact, the old woman never offered a friendly greeting to her customers, nor did she attempt to maintain close ties with her neighbors. She always went out alone and was often seen sitting by herself in the empty restaurant, staring listlessly into space. Seoyeong said it was unlikely Bokhee's Kitchen had any regular customers, and before their falling out she had only gone to the restaurant once or twice a month just because they were in the same building.

Despite the fact that Seoyeong's words were still fresh in my head, I found myself slowly approaching the glass door of Bokhee's Kitchen. It must have been the candlelight. The flame broke into many flickers of light, big and small, and soon illuminated one part of my memory.

Light, lights. Candles on a cake. Someone carrying that cake into a darkened hospital room, drawing the attention of the people standing around in twos and threes drinking wine and beer. Henri had turned fifty-eight that day. It was also the day before he was discharged from the hospital with the understanding that he would forgo further treatment. Lying on his side, Henri had begun a long description of the film he had always wanted to make but never got around to, when he asked for Lisa. When it came to helping him up, he preferred his wife over his daughter. Lisa, who had been standing awkwardly in the corner of the room like an uninvited guest, hurried over to Henri's side and helped him to the cake. Henri's friends, most of them unknown film directors, extras, and crew whose talent had not yet been discovered, gathered around him. Balloons floated around the ceiling and when someone put a party hat on

Henri's shaved head, laughter erupted here and there, but underneath was the sorrow of the last birthday party to be followed by a final farewell. The clicks from the digital and cell phone cameras, the applause, the careful start of the birthday song, and the intermittent sniffles—Henri listened to all these sounds with a peaceful look, took a breath so deep it looked as if the cheeks on his gaunt face nearly touched, then blew out. All the candles went out.

This was my last memory of Henri.

On impulse, I opened the door to Bokhee's Kitchen. All I wanted was to have a warm meal by candlelight under the protective presence of the enormous shadow. At the sound of the clanging door chime, the old woman turned around.

# 4

Henri saw his first movie at the cinema when he was twelve. He received the movie ticket as a birthday present from his mother. His mother and younger sister stayed in the lobby while Henri climbed the steps into the hall alone, his hand holding tight onto his ticket. He would have looked back several times until he was through the doors.

That day, Henri was so overwhelmed by the new world called cinema that he could hardly breathe. It wasn't the content of the movie. A boy of twelve, he wasn't able to fully understand the plot or character dynamics of the American Western he saw that day. The moment of discontinuation when the actor disappears off-screen, independent of the light projected onto the screen, captivated him. Where did he go? Where did she go? Where are they living their uncharted, off-script life? As he watched the movie, he became fascinated with the story unfolding off-screen. It was a realm of the imagination that existed parallel to the story on the screen but unprovable, like the path unchosen that might have led to another life. When he came out of the cinema, Henri knew he could never return to a time when he did not know film.

But the time he spent growing up wasn't smooth sailing. Rather, it was absolutely wretched. His mother was an immigrant born in Turkey. His French father, who'd left as soon as Henri's younger sister was born, never sent them child support. When Henri reached adolescence, he had to help his mother support the family, so his aspiration to attend college and study film remained buried in his heart. He did odd jobs at restaurants and laundromats, cleaned bathrooms in public buildings, and read film theory books during breaks throughout the day. On weekends, he went to the cinema alone and watched two or three films.

Time passed. Henri's mother remarried and his younger sister came of age. Henri packed his few possessions and moved to Paris. It was time to fulfill something he had been planning for a long time. Now in his mid-twenties, he attended a private film academy with the money he was able to save by living in cheap boarding houses. The people he met at that time became lifelong friends and project partners. Henri formed a film production collective with them, and together they made experimental independent films by taking turns being director, staff, and actor. He worked in restaurants and laundromats and cleaned bathrooms in Paris as well, but it cost money to make a film so Henri was still poor. He was poorer than he had ever been in his life, but the poverty did not make him despair. Being poor was nothing compared to the scant opportunities and dreadfully persistent bad luck. Henri's films were never screened in a cinema, he was never invited to a film festival, and the screenplay he revised numerous times did not attract any investors. Just once, news of a famous actor set to star in Henri's film brought in financing, but Henri underwent great despair when the investors pulled out because the actor had changed his mind. Ever since he had arrived in Paris, Henri had always lived like this.

That was as far as he got.

When I finished high school and was preparing to move into the university dormitory—the day I became independent from Henri and Lisa—Henri sat among the boxes in my room and told me this story. *A roller coaster ride of failure and despair, a life wholly his to bear that nobody did or could compensate for—that was my father's life,* I was thinking to myself as I packed in grim silence when Henri called quietly, "Nana." I looked up and he said, "That is life."

Young Henri in his mid-forties, long before the cancer cells had been detected, gave me a faint smile that day, but I could not bring myself to smile back.

Henri didn't know, but from that day on I started thinking about the life off-screen as well. The screen I was looking at projected my own life onto it, not a film, but in any case I had inherited Henri's film gene.

Off the screen—that is to say, outside of my life—was Munju. Suppose there was a Munju who had stayed in Korea and aged at the same pace as Nana in France—two parallel lives weren't completely impossible. On special days, when I was in a good mood, when I kept questioning my good mood until it gave way to a hateful memory, on days when I was overcome, without reason or context, by the premonition that everyone I knew would abandon me, I summoned Munju off the screen as one would reach for a first aid kit. I liked thinking about Munju. Or rather, I thought about her because that was all I could do.

Munju's upbringing and occupation, when she first fell in love, how many people she had gone out with, whether she had a spouse or children—these changed each time I thought of her. But I was certain about a few details: Munju tended to keep her eyes on the ground when she walked; she had trouble throwing things away, so her house was always messy and cluttered with useless objects like rusty rings and broken eyeglass frames; she could not go a single day without reading, and she was addicted to reading everything, including flyers and the recipes on the backs of pasta boxes. Munju and I had an endless list of things in common. Munju also got a stomach ache that lasted all day if she drank cold water on an empty stomach, and if she had tuna, herring, mackerel, or any other fatty fish, she would break out into hives on her chin and neck. Laughter like ascending notes; curling up into a small ball when overwhelmed by despair; and anticipating the end of all relationships, no matter how close—these were all qualities I shared with Munju.

Munju sometimes walked on and on in cold silence. When the phantom sound of train wheels rang in her ears, Munju could do nothing but walk. Soon she would find train tracks in her surroundings. The scenery materialized around her: crushed stones laid under the tracks, grass sprung up on the sides, and a breeze tousling the green blades. As Munju walked, she never looked back, and I didn't try to make her. Besides, I had seen her face—Munju was another me, her face and expressions also mine.

Train tracks . . .

The hazy train tracks that Munju followed endlessly in my mind now stretched before me as a real structure with clear form. On my third day in Korea, which was also the day we shot the opening scene of the film, I stood on the platform at Cheongnyangni Station.

*Strange,* I said to myself. It really was strange. The Cheongnyangni Station tracks that my mind had assembled based on a vague memory was a rundown, abandoned platform from which a long single track stretched on forever. But the platform I encountered was modern and complex. Besides, there were two tracks on each side of the platform, so the image of one long track was nowhere to be seen.

The fact that the platform and tracks, which always morphed into something different each time I pictured it, actually existed as a fixed structure; the fact that it was a real space frequented by real people with warm bodies, with individual expressions and voices—it felt like something out of a dream. If it was a dream, it would be remembered for its sounds—footsteps, wheels of suitcases, announcements of train numbers, destinations, and departure and arrival times ebbing, flowing, filling up the space around the tracks.

I stared intently at the tracks, then began to take a step and then another. Before long, my feet had crossed the safety line and more than half my feet were over the edge of the platform. I glanced back to see Seoyeong and Soyul discussing something in the script, and Seoyeong's boyfriend—he'd shown up in shabby sweats as Seoyeong had warned and introduced himself as "Eun"—gazing up at the changing letters and numbers on the arrival board with the light panel leaning next to him.

Without thinking, I climbed down from the platform and stood in the middle of the tracks. The platform came up to my knees. Passersby gave me strange looks, and some were startled enough to stop. The murmurs brought Seoyeong, Soyul, and Eun rushing toward me. I looked at them and unfolded the construction paper sign I had tucked under my arm. "문주," "Munju" was written on cream-colored paper in my unpracticed handwriting. This was a sort of prop I had made with Seoyeong the previous evening.

"It's okay." I pointed up at the arrival board, which indicated that the next train wasn't coming anytime soon. "It's okay. Film now. Quickly."

Soyul was the first to move. She extended the boom toward me, prompting Seoyeong, who had been staring blankly between me and the arrival board, to break out of her trance and climb down onto the tracks to start shooting. Eun shouted at Seoyeong to forget filming and come back up to the platform immediately, but when Seoyeong said every moment of delay only increased the risk, Eun took a few steps back and lifted the lighting panel. It was impossible for them to miss—that for a wanderer who had lived like a floating speck of dust, the perilous tracks were more grounding than the platform. Besides, for this particular wanderer, the tracks represented her identity.

The summer breeze carried the bitter smell of grass as it passed over the tracks.

The first shot was safely completed, but no one smiled until we had left the platform. The moment Seoyeong said it was a relief we got the shot before the station staff came running, Eun tore into her.

"Not having proper control over the hazardous elements on set is the biggest negligence a film director can commit, and can sometimes be a crime," Eun shouted.

Seoyeong became angrier at Eun for getting angry, and Soyul, looking tired, did not say a word. The place where I was abandoned and found was on the tracks, not the platform, so I couldn't help but step down onto the tracks in that moment. But it was wrong of me to have acted impulsively and not discussed the idea with them first.

I stopped Seoyeong and Eun, who were walking ahead of me each on their own, and said, "That wasn't right of me." After apologizing, I explained myself; the two of them gave me the same look at the same time, their expressions communicating something between disconcertion and guilt.

The icy atmosphere had not completely thawed, but we still had to have lunch together. It was Seoyeong's rule to buy the actors and staff a meal on filming day. As soon as we finished our udon and kimbap at a small restaurant near

Cheongnyangni Station, Soyul rushed off to catch a bus to her part-time box office job at the cinema. Eun and I took the boom and recorder Soyul had rented for the shoot and followed Seoyeong into the subway. All of the film equipment except for the camera was rented by the hour at the filmmakers' guild in Chungmuro. Eun said they ought to return it as soon as possible.

"You're right. It's not right of me to waste budget," Seoyeong quickly replied.

I realized only then that they had already made up and were using the phrase "not right of me" to playfully tease me. Just before Eun got off the train to transfer to Line 4 to return his lighting panel and the equipment Soyul had rented as well, he handed me a neatly folded napkin. On the napkin bearing the restaurant's logo was the Chinese character "銀." He explained that the character referred to the material that white mineral jewellery and coins are made of—silver. I remembered asking him at lunch what "Eun" meant. Leaning against the wall of the rattling subway car, I studied the napkin for a long time.

Seoyeong and I got off at Hapjeong Station.

Hapjeong was where the coffee shop that served as Seoyeong's workplace and project studio was located. Seoyeong worked at the small coffee shop three days a week and often dropped in on her days off to work on her screenplay or put together scripts.

Seoyeong had shared this with me the night before when I was writing "Munju" on the construction paper.

According to the dictionary, Hapjeong was home to a large well with an especially populous clam colony, which is where *hap* (蛤) came from. This turned into the comparatively simple *hap* (合) during the Japanese occupation, and eventually became the "Hapjeong" (合 井) of present day. One interesting fact was that the well wasn't made to procure water for daily use, but dug specifically to wash the blood off the sword that executed Catholics. Being Catholic in the late Joseon dynasty must have been a crime punishable by death.

On our way to the coffee shop, I told Seoyeong about the origin of "Hapjeong" that I had found online the night before. Seoyeong replied that she hadn't known about the name but was aware of the cathedral and memorial for the martyrs in Hapjeong. I thought about how I had never cared about the origins of the arrondissements in Paris, nor had it ever occurred to me to care. When I said to Seoyeong that I would like to go see the site of the large well, if it remained, she said there was no way it was still there. With the price of land in Seoul, the well would have been filled to build a high-rise.

·

When we reached the coffee shop, Seoyeong put up the Open sign, which was lying flat on the ground, and unlocked the glass door. The coffee shop officially opened at ten in the morning, but she had received permission from the owner to open later, after our filming. As soon as we entered, Seoyeong brought out the coffee beans and washed the fruit to prepare for the day's customers, while I sat at the wooden L-shaped table that was an extension of the bar.

"I looked in the dictionary of Chinese characters and found over a hundred characters for 'mun' and over two hundred for 'ju.' Of course, 'baby quail—*mun*' and 'sound of panting ox—*ju*' are very unlikely possibilities."

Seoyeong shared her findings on the other side of the bar as she washed and dried cups, spoons, and plates, and I wrote *Munju, Munju, Munju* on the table with my finger over and over again. In my head, it felt like twenty thousand different houses had been built and knocked down every time there was a new possibility for the meaning of Munju. When I carefully suggested that "dust" might be the correct meaning of *mun,* Seoyeong pretended to have forgotten about that definition.

"Dust? Oh, you mean the second meaning we found in the dictionary. That's just what it says in the dictionary. It's uncustomary to use 'dust' in a person's name."

Seoyeong put the script for the second scene and the cold lemon tea I had asked for on the bar. I did not agree or disagree with her as I looked at the script. Seoyeong and I had plans to visit the Nazareth Orphanage, where I was homed for close to two years. The orphanage, named for the place where Jesus spent his childhood, was still in operation, but Sister Veronica, the nun who was director of the orphanage when I was there, had left.

While it was unlikely anyone would remember me, Seoyeong had gotten in touch with the Nazareth Orphanage in Incheon once she had received word that I would come to Korea, and she had apparently gotten permission to film there as well. Seoyeong seemed hopeful that making our case in person would give us a chance to get in touch with Sister Veronica.

*Clang*, rang the door chime, and two customers who looked like university students came in. They ordered two cups of hand-drip coffee, giving Seoyeong a lot to do. I picked up my script and bag and got off the bar stool. I said a brief goodbye and was walking to the door when I suddenly became curious as to why she had climbed down to the tracks with me at Cheongnyangni Station.

"Oh, that scene had to be shot from the eye level of the actor. And I wanted to see what the actor was seeing too," Seoyeong answered, pouring hot water into a kettle with a long, graceful spout.

She would not have seen it because she happened to be looking down, but I laughed momentarily. Or rather, I think I did.

Outside the coffee shop, everything as far as the eye could see was bathed in summer light. Like a drop of green ink spreading in a small earthen bowl, the summer seeping through my body would grow thicker. This meant that Wooju's bones, blood, organs, and skin would ripen like fruit. I got in a passing cab and as soon as I sunk back in the seat, sleep came over me.

# 5

After nodding off for some time in the cab, I looked out the window and saw that I was already near Seoyeong's place. I bought some peaches at the fruit stall and was walking up to Seoyeong's apartment when I saw Bokhee—ever since I'd eaten at Bokhee's Kitchen two days earlier, the "old woman" had become Bokhee to me—squatting in front of the restaurant. With a hose coming out of the kitchen in the back, she was washing bulky items like large plastic containers, trays, and plates. I walked over and handed her the peaches, saying I bought them to share with her. She squinted up at me because of the sun and smiled, then washed each peach carefully and dried it with a dishtowel.

Unlike Seoyeong's account of the old woman, I found Bokhee to be caring and curious. Since the night of the power outage when I, drawn by the candlelight, came into her restaurant, she seemed interested in me. When I asked her to make me anything that wasn't too spicy, she brought me a clear soup. She set the table with rice and side dishes, then somehow invited herself to sit with me. She said the soup was called baeksundubutang—white soft-tofu soup. I was exasperated that my morning sickness, which had let up, was back, perhaps because of the jet lag. But a few spoonfuls of the hot tofu soup had settled my stomach. This was proof that Bokhee's cooking agreed with me. Sitting across from me, Bokhee had poured me water, pushed the side dishes closer to me, and when I was almost finished with my rice, brought me another bowl. Bokhee smiled each time our eyes met. When she smiled, the loneliness and rage in her expression faded, bringing sadness to the surface instead. If a tendency to pick at the wounds in the heart had taken the form of a human face that had aged harshly over time, it would look like her. I thought of the train conductor's mother. Her sideways stares, her heavy sighs each time I sat down at the table to eat, her hushed reproach at the train conductor as she stole glances at me, and . . . and how she washed me every evening, often took me to the market, and when the neighborhood kids called me names like "beggar" or "orphan," she would always come running from wherever she was and shoo them away. The memory of the day she kept wiping her nose with her fists while she braided my hair also came into focus. The train conductor stood in the corner of the yard smoking cigarette after cigarette and then took my hand, saying it was time to go. She then suddenly grabbed and hugged me. Her tears were getting on my new dress, which was my only worry at the time. *Be well, no matter what. Be well,* she had said through tears. I didn't know what it was to say goodbye, but I knew for sure in that moment that I would never see her again. It was sad, but strangely I did not cry.

That must have been why. I saw the train conductor's mother in Bokhee's face, and because I knew that she had looked after someone else's child as well, I could allow myself to be recklessly honest. Perhaps owing to my awkward Korean, Bokhee cautiously asked me if I came from overseas, which was all the invitation I needed to give her my life's story. I told her about being adopted to France thirty-five years ago, my life in Paris now, and that I was visiting Korea at the request of the young film director living on the third floor. They were only abridgments of long stories, but this was the first time I had impulsively unloaded my personal history onto someone I hardly knew.

"You know the word *jeil?* 'Number one'—*jeil!* The number one person I'm most grateful and sorry to . . . you look like that person. Especially around the eyes and mouth. I was so surprised," was Bokhee's reaction to my confession. She began talking to me like I was a child when I told her I came from overseas. Her eyes grew big and her mouth opened wide to act out "so surprised." I had to laugh. Bokhee gazed at me with her chestnut eyes as I laughed. The kindness she was showing me—I felt its size and volume could be measured by hand. The kindness was inspired by the child Bokhee had once looked after, I was sure of it.

"What does Bokhee mean?" I asked as I paid for the meal. Since my arrival in Korea, meeting someone new and asking what their name meant had turned into a kind of ritual.

"Both 'bok' and 'hee' mean 'you are blessed.' Lucky, you know?"

"So 'Bokhee' is 'lucky' and 'lucky'?"

"Yes, that's right."

When I nodded to show her I understood, Bokhee squeezed my hand and told me to come again soon.

"Let me know any time you want to eat something. Anything. All. Every, every, okay?"

Anything. All. Every, every. The words chosen by this woman who was lucky and lucky had warmth in them, and I finally felt like I had come home. Two nights earlier, on my first night in Seoul, I had thus met Bokhee.

—

I was sitting at an empty table in the hall biting into one of the peaches Bokhee had thoroughly washed, when I heard a voice call, "Bokhee!" An old woman who appeared to be Bokhee's peer was coming up the street pulling a cart filled with a loose stack of cardboard boxes, bottles, and plastic. Bokhee leaned on her knees and picked herself up with a groan to greet her, and the two of them sat side by side under the restaurant awning. They were about the same height, but Bokhee seemed plumper next to the skin-and-bones old woman. The sharp difference in body type made me even more curious about the origins of their friendship. Bokhee produced a pack of cigarettes from her apron, one of which the old woman took, lighting it up and sucking in until her cheeks dimpled, and all the while I could not look away while she smoked the cigarette with such craving. As the old woman smoked, Bokhee looked back at me every now and then as if to make sure I was okay, and smiled gently when our eyes met. When the old woman was done with the cigarette, Bokhee pressed the rest of the pack in her hand and loaded the neat pile of plastic containers that were drying in the shade onto her cart.

When the old woman left with her cart, Bokhee gathered the remaining trays and containers and came back inside. When I offered her a piece of peach, she waved me off saying she couldn't eat hard peaches because of her bad teeth and hurried into the kitchen. I heard the clanging of pots and pans, and Bokhee soon appeared with two bowls containing noodles. My morning sickness had vanished in two days, leaving me curious and in awe of all the food in the world; Bokhee's cooking had much improved my appetite. Bokhee's noodles were made with a watery kimchi called *dongchimi* that had a clear, cool, savory broth. I was eating eagerly with my poor chopstick skills when she put some of her noodles in my bowl and gently chided me not to eat so fast or I would get a stomachache. I coughed and took a sip of water. Why? Why did I choke up at such an ordinary remark?

"Why, don't you like the noodles?" Bokhee asked. She was looking at me with genuine worry. Maybe I started to tell Bokhee about that dish then because I felt so close to her in that moment. Or maybe I thought of those meaningful words—*Anything. All. Every, every*—in just that moment. There was probably also the practical reason that a woman who had run a restaurant for almost ten years would be familiar with the sugar-coated purple food with red bean filling that looked like a flattened dumpling.

Bokhee listened to my description and said she could make it if she saw a picture. "Bring a picture of it next time," she said. Maybe Bokhee didn't know about it either. I hadn't found it on any menu anywhere in Korea yet. I picked up my chopsticks again, and Bokhee watched me in hesitant silence for a moment before asking, "By the way, have you ever been to this country called Belgium? You said you came from France. I saw on the map that Belgium is right next to France. You must have been there, right?"

Traveling to and from Germany or the UK, I usually took a cheap train that transferred in Belgium, a country that had come to be a big transit hub for me. When I replied that I had been there countless times, Bokhee pulled out a photo from her apron. It seemed like the picture had been taken with a camera and processed in a darkroom. Bokhee had been carrying around this photograph, so old and tattered it would not have seemed out of place in a museum, looking for a chance to show it to me.

"It's a girl," I said, taking a close look. This was the child Bokhee had looked after, the one who looked too fundamentally different from me to be, as Bokhee said, "number one" like me.

Was Bokhee seeing something I didn't see? I had no way of knowing.

"She was seven in the picture. She's all grown up now with a job and a family . . . I suppose. So what do you think? Do you remember seeing a kid who looks like that in Belgium? Someone similar, maybe?"

I looked up from the photo and slowly shook my head. Beneath her sagging eyelids, Bokhee's chestnut eyes were quivering. I sensed in that moment that there was a history between Bokhee and the child that went beyond a temporary charge, and that Bokhee had been missing this child for a very long time. Even after I told her that I had never seen this face before, I kept looking at Bokhee, who felt my eyes on her, put the picture away, and said something unexpected: "That was the first kid I caught."

"The kid you caught?"

"When the kid came out into the world, I pulled her out, wiped the blood and vernix off her, and cut her cord."

"You worked at an obstetrician's office?"

"I did other things besides catch babies, similar jobs. For forty years, all over the place . . ."

Bokhee trailed off, bowed her head, and started eating her noodles again. If Bokhee had looked after the girl since birth, then the girl was no different from her own child, I thought to myself. Putting a child up for adoption after raising her like her own was different from temporarily looking after a child who was soon to be put up for adoption. One was protection, the other abandonment. I didn't want to delve further; my life so far had been a struggle to flee from such stories, and besides, now I was with Wooju.

The food tasted bitter in my mouth. I got up without finishing my noodles, mumbled goodbye to Bokhee, and left the restaurant stony-faced. Bokhee asked me to come again, but I didn't answer or look back at her. I just wanted to sleep. A good, long nap would strain all the bad memories through a transparent sieve and let them flow into the realm of subconsciousness. It was strange. Bokhee and I had met as restaurant owner and customer only twice, but I grieved as if I had just been deserted by someone I had known for a long time. With one hand on my stomach, I climbed the stairs thinking the only safe haven left for me was Seoyeong's place, and so the stairway to her apartment seemed like a passageway out of this world. *The shelter for you and me, like the nest of a bird, safe from intrusion or destruction . . .*

# 6

The summer after the year I lived in the train conductor's house as Munju, I was once again a nameless child, this time sent to an orphanage—in my new dress, my hair braided lovingly by the train conductor's mother, with her final wish that I "be well, no matter what." It was a long journey. From Seoul to Incheon by bus, subway, and then bus again, I turned yellow with motion sickness. When we got off the bus for the last time, I squatted by the side of the road and threw up, while the train conductor gently patted my back. What expression was he wearing?

I don't remember.

"The roads around the orphanage were unpaved until

the late 1980s, so you must have walked quite a distance after you got off the bus."

Sister Gemma was sitting on the sofa opposite me with her hands folded neatly on her lap. After recounting my story to her, it came back to me that the orphanage used to be surrounded by makeshift shelters; I did not recall seeing apartment buildings or high-rises there. The orphanage was a remodeled home back then, not the three-story building it was today, once so cramped for space that children had to sleep with their arms and legs on top of each other, not to mention there'd been no gym or library. Sister Gemma told us that there were currently seven children not yet of school age living at the Nazareth Orphanage. The space had gotten bigger and housed only one-fifth of the children now.

Sister Gemma, who looked younger than me, said she had started serving as the director of the Nazareth Orphanage two years ago, when Sister Veronica moved to a convalescent home run by the Catholic Church. The convalescent home was in a port city called Mokpo, which meant that Sister Veronica was much farther away than Seoyeong and I had expected. But the real misfortune wasn't the location of the convalescent home, but the illness Sister Veronica suffered from: dementia caused by depression. There was little chance that a dementia patient would remember an orphan she'd sent over to France thirty years ago, or the temporary guardian who'd brought her to the orphanage. Seoyeong must have reached the same conclusion, as she couldn't hide her alarm when she heard about Sister Veronica's affliction.

Sister Gemma said she had prepared something for me and pulled out a large folder from her desk. The old folder contained my "Child Card," which included my health records and adoption status under the name "Esther Pak"; orphan identification and independent family register; and a copy of the adoption papers signed by "Pak Yeonghee," Sister Veronica's given name. There was no mention of the train conductor in any of the documents. As I combed through every page, I was reminded after all this time that my family name was Jung when I was "Munju" and that my name had changed from Jung Munju to Esther Pak upon joining the orphanage. For about two years, I was Esther Pak. I had inhabited that name for longer than "Jung Munju," but I had formed no fondness or attachment to it because life at the orphanage had left me with no experience that was mine alone. Similar names, fixed schedules, the same amount of deficiency and anxiety allotted to all the orphans, Sister Veronica's and many other adults' rote and customary gestures of affection, and children adopted overseas and sent away periodically to leave an empty space that would soon be filled by new children—these routine cycles had numbed me.

Seoyeong came over with the main camera and got a close-up of the document I was looking at, while Eun stood a step away to get a full shot of me and Sister Gemma. Eun must have rented a second camera instead of the lighting panel because we only had indoor shoots scheduled for the day. Soyul, as she had at Cheongnyangni Station, was careful to stay out of the frame while holding the mic toward the table. The mic was shaped like a hunting rifle and mounted on a tripod, not the boom we used for outdoor shoots.

"'Yeonghee Pak' is Sister Veronica's secular name. During her time at Nazareth, she gave orphans without family connections first names from the Bible and her own last name as their family name. Something small she did to give them a sense of family."

Sister Gemma was quiet for a moment and then said, "And in that sense, I think . . ." She adjusted her glasses and chose her words carefully. "I am certain that the train conductor who brought you went by the last name Jung. I understand he gave you the name 'Munju Jung'? I think he would have wanted to come and get you later. It's very rare for someone to voluntarily foster a lost child for more than one year."

I was at a loss for words. I could not get my head around any of it. When the silence grew heavier, Seoyeong put down the camera and asked Sister Gemma on my behalf, "Can you think of anyone from Sister Veronica's days who might remember the train conductor's name or address?"

"I know there was another sister, but she left the church long ago and I've never met her," Sister Gemma said. "I don't have her contact info, either. I think the police might be able to help you better. A lost child has to be reported at the police station first, even if a family kindly takes the child in. He would have left his information when he filed the report."

Seoyeong bowed her head in thought. Looking down at the floor with a serious expression, she seemed to be sorting through details she may have missed until she saw Soyul signaling at her. She lifted the camera back onto her shoulder and focused the lens on me. I could tell that the orphanage scene would end with a close-up of my baffled face slowly fading out.

While Seoyeong was out filming B-roll of the orphanage with Soyul and Eun, I slowly walked down the hall outside the director's office. Countless picture frames hung on the hall and lobby walls, all pictures of children who had come through the Nazareth Orphanage. I found a familiar face on the landing between the stairwell and the lobby and stopped. It must have been taken right before I went to France. Eyes round and wide in surprise and lips slightly parted, there was Esther Pak/Munju Jung at age seven. Leaning far back, I looked up at the picture for a long, long time until my neck hurt.

Outside the building was just a parking lot paved with cement, no yard where forty-odd children used to play ball or skip rope. Even then, the yard had no playground, not even a swing set, but there was a lot of dirt and sand and large trees that had provided airy shade. Somewhere in the yard, I had buried a pocket mirror. It was the morning I left for France. "If you get on the plane and take a long nap on the clouds, you'll be in France. The bald man and tall woman you met once at the orphanage two months ago will be waiting for you at the airport," Sister Veronica had explained kindly.

As was customary on the day before a child was leaving the orphanage, a small party was held in the evening. We prayed together, shared treats like cake and bulgogi, and all the remaining children kissed the child who was about to leave. I remember rubbing the cheek that had been kissed by so many children with the back of my hand, then going to bed at the same time I always did, but lying awake until daybreak. When I began to hear birds and light filled the windows, I secretly got up and went out to the yard with the pocket mirror, my most prized possession. I squatted on the ground and gazed down at it. A dark, hazy part of my life was in that object. I dug as deep as I could with my hands and buried the mirror, or rather my reflection. Was it because I buried this image of myself here all those years ago that I could later imagine another, parallel Munju in Korea going through life at the same pace as me?

"Here you are," Sister Gemma said. She was standing behind me, anxious to tell me something. "I have a favor to ask of you."

She took a step toward me and said, "Actually . . . Sister Veronica is not in good shape. She and I worked together for ten years, but she doesn't recognize me. The symptoms appeared so suddenly, and the disease is progressing so quickly that it's come as quite a shock to all of us."

"Do you mean she suddenly lost her memory?"

"Well . . ."

Sister Gemma seemed at a loss, then glanced around to make sure no one was listening. "No one knew that Sister Veronica was sick until the incident happened that day," she said in a hushed voice. "Her symptoms had been kept under wraps until one evening she tore down and smashed all the sacred objects in her room, and cut her arms and thighs with one of the shards."

*Jésus!* Lisa's cry echoed in my ear as I listened to Sister Gemma. The day Henri and Lisa found out from the doctor that his cancer was back and had spread all over his body, Lisa had come home drunk, opened the wardrobe, the refrigerator, and the bathroom door in turns and shouted into them, veins popping on her neck, "Jesus! You fucking son of a bitch!"

Henri was in the hospital, so I was the only witness. Lisa never spoke unless necessary and rarely broke out of her hunched posture; she had never acted as hysterically as she had that day. *Like Munju and Nana,* I thought to myself as I pictured Lisa on that day after all this time. Sister Veronica and Lisa's lonely struggles, which were skilfully hidden until one day they exploded, seemed like mirror images of each other. Their laments were nothing more than empty threats against a powerless and indifferent god.

Unlike Sister Veronica, Lisa was not driven to the edge, thanks to Henri. She was six foot two, big-boned with a raspy voice and not a single curve on her body. People treated Lisa like a giant in a land of dwarves, but to Henri she was a little sparrow on his shoulder. He always kept a careful eye on Lisa and his touch was never anything but gentle. I believe it was these memories of him that helped Lisa cope with the loss of Henri and make a secure return to life as usual.

"So the favor I want to ask of you is, well . . . please don't go to see Sister Veronica. She wouldn't have wanted the children she looked after as her own to see her in this sick, frail state. Knowing Sister Veronica, I can guarantee it."

I told Sister Gemma that I would accept her request, that I had no right to refuse. She nodded, and as she turned to go, I blurted out, "Thank you."

"Me? For what?"

"For believing. The train conductor who saved me."

"Oh . . ."

Sister Gemma didn't seem to understand exactly what I was grateful to her for, and I didn't explain. Her speculation that the train conductor meant to take me back was wrong, but no one besides me needed to know that. In that moment, I saw that I would no longer be able to run from the feeling I had that day I buried the mirror in the yard. My little chest was seething with bitterness and I vowed never to look him up, not even if I became extremely successful and so famous that everyone in the world knew who I was. Because the one person who'd believed more fiercely than anyone that the train conductor would come back for me, was me. But until the very day I left for another country, he did not once call me at the orphanage. How I was, where I was and what I was up to, or even if I was dead or alive—he didn't care. After he left me at the orphanage, he never came to see me again.

After an hour together on the subway from Incheon to Seoul, Seoyeong went to a coffee shop with Eun to come up with a new sequence for the film, and Soyul went to her ticketing job as always. I took the bus to Seoyeong's neighborhood and read every store sign carefully as I walked along the street. According to Google Maps, there were three obstetricians around Noksapyeong Station. I hoped to get a checkup at one of them before I returned to France.

The first place reeked of antiseptics so I walked out right away, but I immediately filled out the patient form at the second clinic. The office was small, but the waiting room felt like a pleasant living room, and sitting there was like being invited into someone's home.

A few tests later, the doctor said that Wooju was sixteen weeks old, 10.2 centimetres in length, and weighing a little over 120 grams. Swirls of downy hair were starting to cover them from head to toe, they had genitals and eyebrows, and they urinated every three or four hours. The doctor explained that the forebrain would begin to develop, which would send my feelings to Wooju, who would feel as I feel.

"I see you're from France. Do you have an emergency contact in Korea?" the doctor asked, looking through my file.

"I am my contact. There is no one else."

The doctor looked conflicted, but she didn't ask any questions and only reminded me to take my prenatal vitamins. By the time I came out of the exam room, the short video of the ultrasound had been sent to my phone. The hospital staff also gave me a small booklet for recording the health of the mother and changes in the body until delivery. I took my wallet out of my bag to pay for the checkup and a crumpled napkin fell out. When I looked at the Chinese character for *Eun* written on the napkin, an image of Dennis's hand I had forgotten was slowly reconstructed like an object on a screen when a film is being rewound. The shape of his hand, the lines, and the angles of the tendons all grew more vivid.

Where were we? Probably a pub near the theater. Dennis was an actor who had just entered the industry. He had come to see a performance of the play I had written, and wound up going out for drinks with us at the invitation of a director who was a mutual acquaintance. He had a way with words, and his infectious sense of humor often had the theater company in stitches. I was half listening to a story he was telling that had captivated everyone present when I happened to look under the table and see his hand holding the napkin so tight his knuckles were white. *You're trying so hard,* I thought to myself. His hands were the physical manifestation of his inner state, not mere extremities of his body. When we were together, I paid closer attention to his hands, more than his facial expressions or tone. Holding tight on to a small object like a napkin meant he was nervous, turning pink meant he was feeling shy, and pale blue meant he was ashamed. The last time I saw his hands, they weren't holding anything, and they weren't pink or blue. His hands remained unchanged as he told me he did not love me anymore, and there was no surer sign that we were through. But our paths naturally crossed often after we broke up, and on some of those days we spent the night together without expectations or promises. If he was selfishly using me, then I was doing the same. We were open about our loneliness, but we did not use it as an excuse to look for a future in each other, and I was glad for it.

A few days before I came to Korea, after I found out about Wooju, I ran into him. It was at the retirement performance of an old actor we both knew. After the performance, I saw Dennis in the lobby looking around, maybe hoping to find me. I looked at him from a distance and headed out the back entrance. I didn't want Wooju to be a secret child, but I had no intention of going out of my way to reveal them. I was the one who'd chosen Dennis, knowing he did not want a family and the love between us was gone. Dennis and I did not owe each other anything when it came to Wooju. Dennis was not responsible for Wooju, who would be my family without Dennis's permission or agreement, and I would never harbor any resentment toward him.

I put the napkin back in the bag.

On the way back to Seoyeong's, I got vitamins at the pharmacy and assorted vegetables, rice, and rye bread at the supermarket. A murky darkness was soaking through the fading summer light. I was belatedly hungry. A plastic bag in each hand, I steadily made my way up the hill and saw in the distance the lit-up sign of Bokhee's Kitchen.

I walked past Bokhee's Kitchen and was opening the wicket door when I heard Bokhee. "Third Floor, Third Floor," she called, for lack of a better name, and waved me over. I could not gladly accept her invitation. When one doesn't want to know the truth, the most practical thing to do is to avoid the place where the truth will come to light. This had been my long-held belief.

"This won't take long. Come."

I made an excuse about being tired and wanting to rest, but Bokhee was quite eager. I ran out of ways to turn her down, and I didn't want to lie to her about having work to do or calls to answer.

I reluctantly went back to Bokhee's Kitchen and saw a table set with water, silverware, and side dishes. As soon as I sat down, Bokhee went into the kitchen, and shortly after a nutty smell began drifting into the hall. Bokhee emerged from the kitchen with a plate, and my jaw dropped—it contained a neat row of the brownish-purple, flat, dumpling-shaped food I had told her about.

"Is this . . . how . . . ?"

Bokhee roared with laughter and sat down in front of me.

"Ah, it was nothing. I thought about what you described, and I knew right away. Surprise, you know? This is a surprise. By the way, do you know what this is called?" When I recovered from my shock long enough to shake my head no, she leaned in and enunciated one syllable at a time, "Su, su, bu, kku, mi. Su, su, bu, kku, mi.

"Yes, susubukkumi," she said. "There's a grain called susu. In Gangwondo—it's a place you find if you keep going east from here—there are lots of mountains and badlands unsuitable for growing rice. But susu grows well in badlands, so people made this with it."

Listening to Bokhee's articulate explanation, I could tell that she had put much thought into describing the word to me in the easiest terms possible. *Susubukkumi, susubukkumi,* I said in my head as I picked one up and took a bite, feeling the sound of rain, the smell of rain-soaked trees, and a voice calling me—"Munju-ya"—ebbing back to me in gentle waves.

"It's delicious," I said in a whisper, my head bowed.

Bokhee gazed at me, then got up to get herself a bottle of soju. She took three sips from the cup, then suddenly asked, "How's Belgium? Decent place to live? If you look different, if your blood is mixed, they don't discriminate? Well, I hear in Europe strange-looking people aren't treated any different, and many different races live together, right?"

"Yes, right."

That was partly a lie. For an outsider, discrimination was a condition one could not escape, and there was no exception anywhere. Bokhee took another sip of soju and said gloomily, "I thought I would make it over there at least once in my life. I've lived to be over seventy and I haven't gotten around to it. Not once . . ."

"The child in the picture, was she . . . ?"

*Was she abandoned for looking different?* I did not ask. Fortunately, Bokhee didn't urge me to finish my sentence. She stared into her half-full glass of soju until I finished my susubukkumi. Glints of the ceiling light reflected off the glass onto her face, showing brief glimpses of how she may have looked as a much younger woman.

That is my only memory of her face, one that I remember to this day.

When I finished the whole plate and put down the chopsticks, Bokhee picked herself up with a grunt, packed the leftover susubukkumi into a foam box, and put it in my bag. Before I could thank her, she swept up the plastic bag from the supermarket containing my rice and rye bread and headed out the door. I wanted to tell her that she did not have to carry them for me, but I could not. Because Bokhee knew. Bokhee, and only she, knew about Wooju.

"You're not supposed to carry heavy things when you're pregnant," Bokhee chided as she stepped out of the hall. I could not decipher the powerful waves of emotion rising in me that moment. *The first considerate act you are receiving is a stranger's hospitality, which you have longed for . . .* Picking up the remaining plastic bag and catching up with Bokhee, I slowly realized why her words had such an impact on me.

When we reached the third floor, Bokhee put down the plastic bags at the door and gestured at me to go inside before she headed down. Hunched over and hanging on to the railing, minding her bad knees as she made her way down one step at the time, Bokhee seemed a familiar sight. I thought of Lisa. The fact that I had not told her about Wooju yet weighed heavily on my mind. As soon as I was inside, I found my phone and dialed her number.

As soon as Lisa picked up, she asked if I was sick. The question came out as a reflex. Ever since Henri's death, she had gotten into the habit of skipping over the greetings and going straight to that question. I told her I wasn't sick, not sick but pregnant, all in one breath.

There was a brief silence. The other end of the line was noisy with big and small ambient sounds, but Lisa's breathing was uniformly muted.

"Oh, lord. Nana," Lisa finally whispered. "I have so many questions, but I don't know what to say right at this moment. I don't . . . Would you give me some time? What if I gathered my thoughts and called you back?"

I laughed and said she could call any time. We exchanged awkward goodbyes at the end of the call, but I understood Lisa. Or rather, I understood what was absent for her.

And then there was that day. About ten years ago, when Henri had his cancer cells removed for the first and last time, Lisa had shared in the hall outside the operating room that she had been medically infertile since before she met Henri, a side effect of taking medication to suppress growth hormones since adolescence. She had never been in love and was ignorant of the act of lovemaking before Henri, and had not considered it a loss. But after Henri, it became a source of great pain. "I've never told Henri as much," Lisa said, looking so cold that I gently hugged her. That day, I vowed to be the last person on earth to understand her. Henri's friends sometimes whispered that Lisa was so inscrutably icy and impossible to read, and I had no recollection of ever getting a sympathetic word from her and often found her reticence hurtful, but I would never break my vow. Lisa was my mom, it was as simple as that.

I carried the plastic bags to the refrigerator. "*Magnificent*," I whispered as I put away the foam box from Bokhee and the groceries from the supermarket. That's what Henri would have said were he alive. With that smile that I adored, that brought out the hidden wrinkles all over his face—on his forehead, between the tip of his nose and his lips, on his cheeks and chin—no doubt he would have said, *Nana, you're going to make me a grand-papa. Magnificent.*

# 7

Ahyeon was located between Sinchon and Gwanghwamun, and not very far from Itaewon or the coffee shop in Hapjeong where Seoyeong worked. The house we were looking for was surprisingly close. On the way to Ahyeon, we passed a block of mostly wedding halls, and on the next block was a mix of realtor's offices, furniture stores, and restaurants. In Ahyeon, one could get married, buy a house, buy furniture to fill it with, and grab a bite all in the same place—a physical representation of a certain phase of life rolled out onto a street.

Seoyeong explained that Ahyeon was in the process of redevelopment into a posh apartment district. Luxury residential buildings towered on the left side of Ahyeon Station, while some old houses and small stores still stood on the right side. According to Google Maps, the guesthouse Seoyeong had found was far down to the right of the station, the less developed side. I followed the map past a few streets and reached the guesthouse. A moving van was parked in the alley. Two men in green vests were loading big and small items onto the truck. I stood and watched them haul a wardrobe, dressing table, and refrigerator bearing the wear and tear of old age.

"The train conductor and his mother don't live there now. I checked it out ahead of time, and now it's a refurbished hanok guesthouse run by a young couple. Before that, a retired doctor owned the house, so I'm guessing the train conductor left a long time ago," Seoyeong had informed me that morning, when she'd called for the first time since the Nazareth Orphanage shoot five days before. This didn't come as a surprise; it was unlikely that a family would live together in the same house for decades. Still, my hands were shaking when I wrote down the train conductor's address, and I could not calm down for some time.

When I got off the phone with Seoyeong, I looked up Ahyeon on the Internet. Originally called Aegogae, the place name was converted to classical Chinese with a similar sound: Ahyeon. *A*—slope. *Hyeon*—hill. During the Joseon dynasty, when corpses had to be taken out of the walled city, Aegogae, which is present-day Ahyeon, is where the children were usually buried. I had spent my one year as Munju in the part of Seoul that had the saddest history, a children's graveyard.

The moving van pulled out, and two wooden chairs placed side by side against the wall came into view. I walked over and sat in one. It was creaky and off-balance. That must have been why they were left behind. I sat back in the chair, looking up at the electric lines. A long, white ribbon caught on the wire and fluttering in the wind seemed like a sign meant only for me—the guesthouse happened to be right under that ribbon.

Seoyeong said that she had been to three police stations near Cheongnyangni Station and two police boxes, but none of them had records of my being found on the train tracks in 1983. Missing-children cases were not organized and managed systematically back then, and paperwork had not been digitized, so there was no way to search through the files. She had all but given up hope when she got a call from Sister Gemma.

"Sister Veronica thought that a child might want to find her parents or that a parent might want to find their child someday, so she kept an unofficial record. She turned it over to Sister Gemma when she went into the convalescent home. After we left that day, she took another look and found the name and address of the person who brought in Jung Munju. She said it was a small miracle that a document written with a ballpoint pen thirty-five years ago was well-preserved enough to make out."

As Sister Gemma had assumed, the train conductor did have the last name Jung. Jung Woosik. Age thirty-one at the time. Next to his name and age were his home address and a phone number that was no longer in service; there was no Chinese character notation of his name or resident registration number. Seoyeong had called the Korea Railroad Corporation and asked for the contact information of a train conductor called Jung Woosik, but they told her there was no train conductor by that name, and that even if there had been, they did not give out personal information. After all that effort, he was still just out of reach. Like the undying city lights in the distance seen from a dinghy drifting from port, unable to drop anchor.

The friendly young couple who owned the guesthouse gave us permission to film. Before the shoot, I took a walk around the hanok that had been renovated into a two-story house. A pleasant arrangement of flowers and shrubs grew in the expanded garden, and a row of soft, peach-colored lamps hung from the eaves. Two foreigners staying at the guesthouse were putting on their shoes on the stone steps, and I could see as real as day my own small sneakers through the tunnel of time. The train conductor and his mother would not have known about this, but I often sat in a tight ball out in front to look at my shoes among the other shoes on the stone steps. The sight filled me up for some reason, the same way I felt after eating a lot of sweet, tasty food. Another name for that feeling was "belonging," one that I was experiencing for the first time in my life.

The sequence was shot in the form of an interview on the front maru of the house. When Seoyeong, outside the frame, asked me a prepared question, I responded within the frame. Soyul was in charge of sound as always, and Eun took over the main camera for Seoyeong.

Seoyeong asked me what I remembered about the exterior and atmosphere of the hanok, memories related to train conductor Jung Woosik, and how I felt the moment I was called "Munju" for the first time. I took my time with the answers.

"If you were to meet Jung Woosik again, what is the first thing you would say to him?"

To Seoyeong's final question, I gazed into the camera without responding right away. It was an awkward pause that I was sure Seoyeong would edit out later.

"I would say, 'Thank you.' But that wouldn't be enough. Nothing I say will be enough. But . . ." After a long while, I continued, "But that gratitude that no words can express is only a partial gratitude. In the past I have also resented him, sometimes even more than my birth mother."

"Why is that?"

"Well." I took another long pause. "Because I was abandoned once again."

Seoyeong did not add any comments. She quietly said, "Cut," and turned off the mic. Eun and Soyul also carefully put down their equipment without a sound. The shoot was over.

We thanked the young couple and headed out as a breeze heavy with moisture rushed past us. Seoyeong said it looked like it was about to rain, which had Soyul and Eun hurrying off to keep the equipment from getting wet, while I followed. Outside the guesthouse, I saw an old woman, maybe older than Bokhee, nodding off on one of the broken chairs by the wall. A wistful weariness came over me; it felt as if I had come face-to-face with my future self, who had lived a whole life in the blink of an eye. I looked back several times as we made our way out of the alley, but the old woman did not wake up. Will the street and all the houses have turned to dust when the old woman wakes from her dream? The alley seemed to reflect a pattern in my present life.

We returned the film equipment in Chungmuro and went over to the coffee shop in Hapjeong for a meeting Seoyeong had requested. The staff working at the coffee shop led us to a more private booth behind a partition. When Seoyeong announced that she would buy us drinks instead of a meal today, Soyul and Eun ordered four bottles of beer.

They were worried about the next scene. The Munju trail had reached a dead end; we didn't have enough footage and what we did have was not in line with the direction of the film. Many suggestions were laid on the table: check out every Jung Woosik over sixty in the country; post the story of my abandonment on the train tracks, alongside a picture of me when I was living in the orphanage, on various Internet sites; and other impractical ideas . . . As night came, the collection of empty beer bottles on the table grew and our meeting lost momentum and came to an end. The three of them had split the beer equally, but Seoyeong was the only one who was drunk. Flushed, she leaned in close to me and, pointing at my still-full glass, asked if I couldn't hold my liquor. Her warm breath smelling of sweet beer felt good on my face.

"No, I've always been too good of a drinker. I'm just keeping it in check now."

"Why, oh, why?"

"Do you really want to know?"

"Of course!"

"Because," I said after a beat, "I'm pregnant."

In that exact moment, Seoyeong jumped up from her seat and ran for the bathroom with her hand cupped over her mouth, with Eun following her. Seoyeong and Eun may not have heard me, but Soyul must have. She avoided my gaze as if to say she hadn't heard a thing, but I did see her flinch. Without intending to, I now shared a secret with Soyul. I thought things might get uncomfortable if Seoyeong came back from the bathroom and asked the question again, so I grabbed my bag and left before she returned. Soyul got up to see me out, but I said I didn't want to be treated like a child and left the coffee shop alone.

On the cab ride back to Seoyeong's apartment, it started to rain again. The sound of the rainfall was amplified as though a volume dial hidden somewhere in the atmosphere had been turned up. I gazed out the window and imagined the white pear blossoms falling on the stables. I pictured the large well in Hapjeong filling up with rainwater and the children's graves of Ahyeon getting wet. Seoul seemed like a city of many dimensions, with a visible layer on top of an invisible one. The lines and colors of the landscape changed with the angles, like the snow globe Henri gave me as a gift when I was young. It was as if I were sitting inside it now.

When I got out of the cab, it was almost eleven at night, but the light in Bokhee's Kitchen was still on. There was a customer, too. Bokhee and a middle-aged male customer sat at separate tables drinking the same soju with their heads hanging in the same way; they looked like passengers on a night train sitting in adjacent cars. Holding up my umbrella,

I walked slowly toward the entrance. I stood there for a while but could not open the door.

I turned around.

I climbed the twenty-seven steps and opened the door, which felt like the last exit out of this world. When I'd entered the apartment, I leaned against the door. It was hard to shake the feeling that on the other side was a film set built for the perfect screenplay that would become the perfect film—as long as outsiders like me kept out of it. My role on that set would have vanished long ago, when I began my life in France as Nana. Then again, I'd long since thought of the outside world in terms of two-dimensional grids—movie screens.

My phone was going off in my bag. I picked it up and heard a familiar voice. The sensor light in the foyer went out. Off-screen, I quietly waited for Lisa's story.

# 8

"Nana, I wanted the last film of my life to be about the beginnings of our family," Henri had said. He was lying on his side, telling me this on his fifty-eighth birthday before someone came in with the cake. I knew that the movie he was going to tell me about would be the last words and testament of Henri Moreno. "It was summer," he continued with a smile, and I drew his hand to my face and rubbed my cheek against his palm like a newborn kitten that had yet to open its eyes.

One summer long ago, thirty-year-old Henri and thirty-three-year-old Lisa were living in a world awash with light. The traffic and caution lights on the road seemed to have been turned on for them, and the round pool of sunlight streaming in through the window first thing in the morning was a spotlight on their romance. They had met earlier that spring at a bookstore on Boulevard Saint-Michel. In the basement, the bookstore had held a screening of an independent film for which Henri had been part of the crew, and Lisa, a middle-school teacher, was one of the eleven people in the audience.

Until Henri went on a trip to Nice with Lisa and ran into a former member of the film community, he believed that this world of light was the realm of love.

The colleague, who was the same age as Henri, wrote screenplays that included scenes from Henri's own scripts from past workshops, so Henri had always felt uncomfortable around him. One day, this colleague had vanished from the community without a word, then sent news that he'd sold a screenplay to a film production company, and around the same time debuted a film that had received a nod from the establishment. Henri froze when he saw the man walking toward him and Lisa. The colleague recognized Henri and walked over and shook his hand. It did not occur to Henri to introduce Lisa as he listened stony-faced to his colleague go on about his new movie. By the time Henri noticed Lisa again, the colleague had already left. At some point, he had let go of her hand. The world had turned dark again as if the power had gone out, and like the first man becoming aware of his nakedness, he could not bear to look at Lisa.

The silence continued back at the hotel. Lisa broke the silence first.

"If you're ashamed of me, we should break up," Lisa said, to which Henri replied in a pained whisper, "Please, Lisa. I was ashamed of you in that moment, which continues to confound me, but I am certain that I am more ashamed of myself for being ashamed of you, and if this shame is real, our love is still valid." She would not have doubted Henri's words. Perhaps she never had a moment's doubt.

She slowly turned around and, for the first time, confessed that she wanted a child. Henri, who knew that Lisa could not have children, gazed quietly back at her. Darkness was seeping in fast where light was fading, but Henri learned when he saw Lisa's tears that a true love does not deny the presence of darkness.

That night, Henri and Lisa decided on two things: they would adopt a girl, and they would call her Nana. Nana was the name of the protagonist in a Godard film they had watched on their first date at an old, rundown theater on the edge of Paris.

"Nana, that is how you came to us."

One person's ambition colliding with an intractable envy, a pivotal point that changed the way two people loved one another. Then, through a black-and-white film at a rundown theater, I came into their world. Hearing about the beginnings of our family once again through Lisa's words brought back the look on Henri's face when he recounted the story to me in the hospital that day, his proud tone, and how he had gazed at me teary-eyed when he was finished.

Lisa said on the phone, "As a result of many coincidences, you met me and Henri by something close to a miracle. Do you understand? Just as the new life is precious to you, you are precious to Henri and me. Now is the time to love yourself more than you ever have. Don't be so hard on yourself, Nana."

I listened quietly.

"Nana, Henri and I felt sad every time you tried to hide that you wanted something." Lisa's voice was as gentle as a whisper and closed the physical distance between us. The time difference between France and Korea seemed to close as well, and the thirty-five years Lisa lived as my mother compressed to a thin sheet that made every moment seem like only yesterday.

Lisa had spoken from the heart, so it was now my turn to tell her about Wooju. I told her what the name meant, when Wooju came to me and when the due date was, and why I had come to Korea. Lisa suggested I come to Montpellier when I returned to France and give birth there, that she would be there for me.

After I got off the phone, I realized Lisa had not asked me anything about the biological father. From the moment she first received the news five days ago, she would have made up a list of things to say and things not to say with the objective of showing support.

The foyer's light came on and went out again. I thought of the days when I was going from minor role to minor role, playing the extra who walked past the lead and going backstage to remove the makeup on my own. I used to think that if Henri died without ever having his film screened at a theater, the backstage green room would be an apt metaphor for his life. I wasn't there for Henri's last moment. My father wanted to spend whatever time he had left with Lisa and Lisa only. The day after his fifty-eighth birthday, he checked out of the hospital and the two of them went down to Montpellier, where he lived another month and died.

Henri died.

Henri died, and it was the end of one act for both Lisa and me. We would never return to the time before his death. I put my career as a stage actor on hold to pursue playwriting in earnest, and Lisa tendered her resignation at school and permanently moved to Henri's hometown and the last place they'd gone on a trip together, Montpellier. In Montpellier, Lisa lived not as a math teacher but as a custodian at a library, and she had not left Montpellier in the last five years. Lisa was a hardworking employee—she was never late or missed work—and when she got off work, she had dinner at the same Vietnamese restaurant where Henri had worked as a server when he was young and then went home. It was a monotonous life, but she was more relaxed than ever, she once told me. Back in Paris, I often pictured the Vietnamese restaurant she stopped by almost every day. A restaurant at the end of the street, red lanterns hanging outside, and the smell of spice in the air. A space that became complete when a towering, lonely woman walked in, a small piece of the world that could transport her anywhere when she was eating there. I would have dinner there after Wooju's birth. Lisa's tone, when she invited me to Montpellier, was detached, but it gave me endless comfort.

Comfort that I wasn't alone.

# 9

"I have an appointment with a train conductor tomorrow. He's the older brother of a college friend, who started working for the Korea Railroad Corporation last year. There's got to be a company directory, so it'll just be a matter of time before we get ahold of Jung Woosik's address or phone number," Seoyeong said the moment I sat down at the bar table.

The train conductor still seemed like the faraway lights of a port city seen from a dinghy drifting out to sea, but I looked at Seoyeong and said it did sound promising. Seoyeong, who was doing everything she could to track down the train conductor and finish her film, reminded me of Henri, and I knew better than anyone that such passion wasn't a gift one saw in another person every day.

As it was lunchtime, Seoyeong paced back and forth between the refrigerator and stove behind the bar to whip up a spaghetti dish with tomato sauce and mushrooms. The tomato sauce tasted generic and factory-made, and the mushrooms were so undercooked they were almost crunchy, but I finished my portion in no time.

Seoyeong laughed without curiosity or suspicion. "I've never seen anyone eat something I made with such enthusiasm," she said. It was clear she hadn't heard my confession a couple of nights ago. I considered trying to tell her again, but thought better of it. Every one of us existed as a result of a woman's pregnancy and childbirth, and there was no reason for me to hide Wooju from anyone, but I didn't want my situation to be a burden on Seoyeong.

Seoyeong was on the late shift, so I left the coffee shop alone. It was late July. The city was at the height of summer, and each day brought record-breaking heat. The sun beat straight down on the leaves, which undulated green waves. I hurried to the subway station because it was too hot and humid to walk.

When I got back to Seoyeong's neighborhood, I walked past a fruit vendor that had on display soft pink peaches, which made me think of Bokhee. Yesterday and the day before, Bokhee's Kitchen was closed so I didn't see her. Since Bokhee's Kitchen was my only way into Bokhee's world, the closed door was like a barrier in the relationship.

I should have been glad for the distance. I had the susubuk-kumi I'd been craving thanks to her, but I had not visited her at the restaurant since then and tried my best not to catch her eye when passing by. If Bokhee showed me the photograph and started sharing the story, the child's history would be restored. And I still had no interest in hearing such stories.

Bokhee's dented restaurant sign came into view. A little further up the road, I saw a wide-open door and a crowd gathered around it. An ambulance siren began to wail. First unbelievably slowly as though it were in slow motion, then a little faster, and then desperately urgent and insistent. I started running but there was no use. The ambulance parked outside of Bokhee's Kitchen was pulling into the main street with a piercing wail before I could get there.

I stood in the road and repeated to myself, *Bokhee, Bokhee.*

It was Bokhee's vegetable supplier who told me which hospital she was taken to. She had come by to collect a late payment when she found Bokhee collapsed on the ground.

"She didn't take my calls, didn't answer the door, so I knew something was off. I called a locksmith to get inside, and there she was, lying in the room behind the kitchen. What could I do? I called an ambulance."

The words rushed out of her, then she chided me to stop dawdling and go check her in at the hospital. She must have seen me dashing toward Bokhee's Kitchen in a panic and thought I was her daughter or niece. When I told her that I wasn't a family member but just a customer, the vegetable supplier's face darkened instantly.

"Oh no. They won't admit her to the hospital, let alone operate on her without consent from a family member or guardian. Do you know anything about her family?"

I said I didn't, to which she responded with a heavy sigh and walked off with the scattering crowd, muttering, "Oh, what about the bills?" Once the crowd dispersed, stillness fell over Bokhee's Kitchen. I stared inside for a long time at the tables and chairs in disarray, then turned around and hailed a cab.

I rushed to the emergency room, but the entrance was crowded and only family members of patients were allowed access. After feeling lost for a while, I found the visitors' registration desk. I told the staff that I was looking for the patient who had just arrived by ambulance from Itaewon-dong and that I didn't know her family name but that her first name was Bokhee.

The staff answered right away that there was no one named Bokhee, but that the patient I just described went by Chu Yeonhee.

"Chu Yeonhee?"

"Chu Yeonhee. What is your relationship with the patient?"

I was at a loss for words. Who was I to Bokhee, or rather, Chu Yeonhee? Why had I rushed to be by her side? But the person at the emergency room registration desk was not looking for a metaphorical answer but an objective one. I decided to lie.

"I live in the same building as Bokhee, I mean, Chu Yeonhee. I came at the request of her guardian, who lives out of town, to check on her status. Can I see her?"

"The guardian sent you?" the receptionist asked, shuffling through paperwork. A conflicted look emerged on her face. They wouldn't be able to get in touch with Bokhee's guardian yet, and she was coming to the conclusion that it would be easier to check the patient in with someone who claimed to be the guardian's proxy than no guardian at all. As I expected, the staff gave me a document to fill out and bade me to bring the guardian as soon as possible.

After signing various documents I walked into the emergency room, where I was overwhelmed by the stench of chemicals, the sound of medical equipment, and patients moaning in pain. Bokhee—she was officially Chu Yeonhee but still Bokhee to me—was in the farthest corner of the emergency room, lying on her back with a ventilator on her face. On the chart hanging at the foot of her bed was the name of the patient and the diagnosis—stroke. I carefully studied Bokhee's face. She looked so peaceful I'd have sooner believed she was asleep than unconscious from a ruptured vein in her head. I pulled down her T-shirt, which had ridden up her midriff, and gathered up the plastic slippers that had been tossed at the bedside. I wanted to do more for Bokhee, but there wasn't anything else for me to do. I also didn't have the right—I was a customer who had eaten at her restaurant only three times. I had a minor role in her life, someone who didn't even know her real name.

I left the hospital and walked to the subway station wondering who the real Bokhee was. I thought of the child in the photo. If the girl had grown up to be my age, and if *she* was the real "lucky and lucky" Bokhee, she would have forgotten the name she had in Korea. She may have had no idea that someone in Korea had opened a restaurant they named after her and that they were still looking at her photo from time to time. *Stroke. Can't be operated on without guardian consent.* The words weighed me down and slowed my steps.

Back at Seoyeong's place, I was getting food out of the refrigerator to make dinner when I spotted the foam box in the freezer. I put the susubukkumi on a plate, microwaved it, and took it to the living room table. With every bite, I could hear the way Bokhee spoke and see the faces she made in clear detail. The way she nudged the side dishes closer to me, watched TV with a bored look, drank soju, shared cigarettes and food with an old woman poorer than her. She was healthy and alive.

I made the sixth and final susubukkumi last as long as possible, and when I had swallowed the last bite, I got up and left the apartment again. I went down to the first floor, pulled at the door of Bokhee's Kitchen, and was surprised to find it open. The locksmith must have forgotten to lock it again. This meant that the door would remain unlocked until the landlord did something about it.

Inside the restaurant, I smelled something familiar in the still air. Flatware, knives, ladles, pots, and other kitchen utensils bearing Bokhee's scent, I thought to myself. I went straight into the kitchen. There was no door to speak of between the dining area and the kitchen, but there was a sliding door made of frosted glass beside the refrigerator. The vegetable supplier had said she found Bokhee in the room behind the kitchen. If she was right, Bokhee's living quarters were beyond that door. And the door indeed led to a narrow passage with a room on one side and a bathroom on the other. Here was another thing I had not known about Bokhee—I could not have imagined that she lived at the back of the restaurant.

I took off my shoes and stepped into her room. The overhead light blinked a few times and went out each time I switched it on, but the table lamp on the shelf came on right away. An amber light filled the room and revealed a fabric closet and plastic dresser, worn-down clothes hanging from nails, and an electric fan with a chipped blade. On the shelf next to the lamp were face lotions in plastic tubs, a tube of lipstick missing its cap, a grimy hand mirror, and a flip phone connected to the charger. My eyes scanned the room and suddenly stopped at one place.

The open ledger on the futon. I sat down and looked through the thick record of transactions, the final item reading, "Boksun giil," followed by words like "rice cake," "mung bean powder," "pear," "apple," and some scrawled numbers. I looked up *giil* on my phone. *The day of someone's death. The day people close to the deceased mourn the death* was the definition, and so I was able to deduce that Boksun and Bokhee were close and that the anniversary of this Boksun's death was this time of year. Most telling of all were the overlapping syllables in their names: *Bokhee, Yeonhee, Boksun.* Was this pattern a clue that would shed light on Bokhee's past? This possibility made her life seem like one big mystery.

"Mystery," I whispered as I lay down. The futon gave off another scent, perhaps a mixture of Bokhee's sweat and tears. The hot air in the room did not cool down after the sun had set, and the insects outside the window were screeching with everything they had. Looking up at the low ceiling gently bathed in orange light, I thought of the loneliness of a soul hardening with time in a coffin under the ground. None other than my own soul looking down at a life consolidated into just a particle of light destined to vanish at sunrise . . .

Was that the reason?

Was that why I thought of those days?

There was a time when I had endlessly thought about death. It was in college, after I went to therapy. The session had lasted only thirty minutes, but for three years, scarcely a day went by when I didn't think about what the therapist had said to me. If I really was neglected in an unbearable environment or abused before I was abandoned on the railroad tracks, the first cells that made me who I was were formed under tragic circumstances. This thought oppressed me. A child that was purely a physiological phenomenon, created as a byproduct of a monetary transaction or violence, an uninvited intruder who came into this world, unwelcome by all. Maybe I had suspected it all along. The therapy was just a catalyst that brought to the fore the possibility I had been denying.

I became an actor to escape these thoughts. As long as I was acting, I could live someone else's life. The stage was, in fact, the only way I could flee from the life I was born into. It was rare for an Asian actress to land a lead role, but when I did, I still had to face the fact that reality was waiting for me outside the theater once the play ended. But I would not have had the strength to bear anything if not for the time I got to spend on the stage. Fortunately, time passed at a sedulous pace and I slowly moved away from the days when death was the only thing on my mind. Or so I believed. There were still days I found myself under the shadow of death. Like the day I remembered hearing from the doctor that Wooju would soon develop their forebrain and feel what I feel. I clenched my fists until my knuckles turned white and flexed my feet, willing my emotions not to flow into Wooju's body. Wound tight, I was about to sit up when my stomach gurgled and I could literally feel a physical movement sweep the inside of my stomach. I froze in place like a boxer stunned by an unexpected jab. The movement became shorter, then longer, and then faded. I carefully rolled onto my side and curled up with my arms around my stomach. The nerves that had wound tight all over my body seemed to relax all at once. *The sign that you are alive, the knock on the door of the world, the small movement of your body coming to me when I need it most, telling me what I most need to hear.*

Wooju's quickening.

# 10

As soon as I got out of the elevator, I saw Soyul standing by the ticket booth, looking around. She had received my call and had come out to find me. It was my first time seeing Soyul, who always wore gender-neutral clothing, in a skirt with a white shirt and tie, which made her appear as a stranger to me. I told her she looked different in lieu of hello, and she smiled shyly, saying she always felt awkward in her work clothes.

I hadn't meant to bother Soyul at work, but I ended up getting in the way anyway. She had to ask a coworker to cover for her for about half an hour. Soyul led me to the roof of the building, where there was a seating area that had been put together like a small garden. Soyul often came here on her breaks. We sat side by side on a bench and had a polite conversation about the weather, the public reception of the film I was going to see that day, and Soyul's job selling movie tickets. After a brief silence, I told her I was curious as to why she was financing this film with money she needed for her own expenses. I had remembered Seoyeong's comment about the staff and the director pooling their money together to make the documentary. Instead of having full-time careers, Seoyeong and Soyul were working part-time jobs to make non-commercial films and Eun was still lost after being discharged from the army, so I supposed that coming up with even a small budget would be a great burden for them.

"Well . . ." Soyul scratched the back of her head as if she were embarrassed, but said firmly, "At the end of the movie, when the end credits roll—I like that moment. I see my name and feel alive. I don't make a lot of money and what little I have saved I spend making movies, but my name in the end credits makes up for it, for now. I don't know how long this will last, though."

Soyul's response reminded me of the Bokhee's Kitchen sign. For Bokhee, the restaurant was her workplace and residence. All the paths she had taken in her life led her to this space, which was for herself alone. All of her labor, investment in property, and time were poured into the restaurant that bore the name Bokhee, perhaps as a way of sending out the message that she was still alive. Was the naming itself how Bokhee—Bokhee to me but officially Chu Yeonhee—chose to prove her existence? And did it make up for her weary life?

Soyul was thoughtful for a moment, then asked, "Are you doing all right?"

Soyul was probably worried about my health. I told her I was doing great and that I felt at peace. That coming to Korea had been an impulse decision, but that I didn't regret it; I'd get through just fine without anyone's help, and I'd be back in France in September at the latest to get ready for the birth. The words rushed out of me as if to reassure her that no one had to feel burdened by my condition. Soyul gazed back at me and told me to feel free to ask for anything. The director and staff had a duty to protect the actors, and I could ask for help whenever I needed it, that I really must.

With a firm look on her face, she said, "I know you're being careful not to be a burden on us, but if Seoyeong or Eun knew, they would say the same thing."

Soyul spoke with certainty, and only then did I slowly come to terms with the fact that I had been yearning for such an assurance.

It was almost movie time, so I went down from the roof. Before I went in, I watched Soyul from a distance as she returned to her post to check tickets and point people to their theater. The reason I'd come all the way to Jongno to watch a movie, instead of going to one of the many theaters in Yongsan, was because I wanted to tell someone with an objective point of view about Bokhee. Should I intervene and make choices that would affect the rest of her life, or should I mind my own business like the stranger I was, who didn't even know her real name, and turn a blind eye to whatever happened to her? The only three friends I had made in Korea were Seoyeong, Soyul, and Eun, and Soyul happened to be more mature than Seoyeong and easier to talk to than Eun. Soyul may not have noticed, but talking to her brought to my attention one important fact: if Bokhee was an actor who had wandered into a scene of my life, I had the duty to protect her as well. Protection was the attitude and action Henri and Lisa, and the train conductor Jung Woosik, took when I wandered into their lives. Rather than turning away, they drew a life closer into their lives.

Soyul's hands began to move faster when a crowd of people flocked to the ticket booth. While I was watching her, I suddenly remembered something. I rummaged through my bag and found the booklet I had picked up at the clinic a week ago. I opened the booklet and in the blank space next to "taemyeong (prenatal nickname)," I slowly wrote *Soyul*. Wooju would exist as a "little chestnut tree" until they came into the world. I felt another movement inside—Wooju must have approved of the name. Ever since the quickening, Wooju reminded me from time to time that they were alive.

—

Bokhee had been moved from the emergency room to the ICU to a regular ward. Fortunately, the staff at the reception desk recognized me and told me that Ms. Chu Yeonhee's guardian had come by to take care of the paperwork. The receptionist must have thought that the guardian had come to pay off the hospital bill at my request because she was much friendlier than when we first met and pointed me to the room Bokhee was in. I had more questions for the staff, most importantly how Bokhee was doing, but people kept pushing to the front of the reception desk and I had no choice but to offer a quick word of thanks and leave.

The in-patient ward was in the building across from the emergency ward. Bokhee was in a two-person room on the thirteenth floor, but when I got there the bed by the door was empty and Bokhee was alone in the bed by the window. I slowly made my way to her, one step at a time. Tubes both translucent and opaque were going in and coming out of Bokhee's body; one was attached to her urine bag. The sight wasn't disquieting, as I had seen Henri lying in his hospital bed with a similar setup. I had learned long ago that food and medicine went into the nose and arm tubes and that urine came out of the tube below the waist. "I can see everything going in and coming out of my body, Nana," Henri had said with a shy smile I could still see as if it were yesterday. "I feel like a cylindrical single-cell organism with a clear entrance and exit."

A nurse came into the room with a fresh set of hospital clothes for Bokhee and greeted me with more enthusiasm than was necessary. She asked if I was the patient's family, and when I gave her a vague answer—"a close neighbor"—her face instantly fell. She seemed young and inexperienced and had a very expressive face. Before I knew it, I was standing by the nurse's side helping her change Bokhee into fresh clothes.

"What's going to happen to Chu Yeonhee now?" I could not help but ask anxiously.

"The doctor's opinion is that there is little chance she'll wake up even if she goes through with the surgery. Besides, the patient had already signed a do-not-resuscitate order. That means we can't give her CPR. We've removed the ventilator, too, as you can see. In this state, she will live about two months at most."

"Then who looks after her until she passes?"

"I was wondering about that myself. It would be better for the patient to be moved to a home or a hospice ward, but the guardian doesn't seem to want to bother. She hasn't picked up the phone since her visit."

"Guardian . . . is she family?"

"She said she was the patient's younger sister."

According to the nurse, Chu Yeonhee's younger sister—no, her name was not Bokhee—went to the nurse's station as soon as she signed the papers and told the nurses not to lose any of the documents because she needed them to have the hospital bills reimbursed from her life insurance. She then left Bokhee in the care of the hospital-appointed shared caretaker and rushed off. The nurse said that cases like these are quite a headache for the hospital staff. She felt uneasy about leaving an unconscious patient alone without a guardian or a full-time caretaker, and said that it would be nice to have someone in the room to at least check on her breathing so that she wouldn't have to die alone. The nurse went on and on to a stranger she had just met.

The nurse picked up Bokhee's hospital clothes, which had been peeled off her body like old skin, and left the room. I looked down at Bokhee. Carefully watching her breathing and searching for signs of imminent death was not simple caretaking or temporary protection. To take on the role was to watch as a life departed from the world and then announce that departure to others. That is, this was the opposite of being witness to Wooju's arrival in this world.

Strangely, the thought of Wooju banished all my doubts and settled the matter immediately. I ran out into the hall after the nurse, and quickly told her that I would stop by whenever I could to check in on Bokhee. Perhaps I had rushed to declare it out loud before I changed my mind. The nurse was delighted and instructed me to page the medical staff at any time if I saw anything was amiss.

I returned to Bokhee's side, and while I was smoothing out the wrinkled bedsheets, her white tofu soup, dongchimi noodles, and susubukkumi came to mind, one after the other. The flavors had irritated or soothed my tongue, my insides, and a part of my heart. Looking back, Bokhee had cooked for me every time I went to see her. In my life, no one had been so interested in nourishing me. Her cooking was always good and reminded me that Korea was my home and my mother's home. If by some miracle she woke up and asked me what I was doing with her at the hospital, I thought I would list those dishes.

*The food was reason enough for me to keep vigil here; because it made you grow, it became sustenance for your blood and bones.*

On the bus back to Seoyeong's I saw a woman my age with a baby sling wrapped across her chest and stomach. My feet led me to her. I was standing in front of her and looking down at the sleeping baby's round head and chubby cheeks when our eyes met. The good-natured woman said that the baby was five months old. I smiled, imagining Wooju one year later, and was surprised when the woman gently ran her eyes over me and asked how far along I was. I had a small bump poking out through a thin T-shirt, but it was undetectable at a quick glance. When I told her I had just gotten to seventeen weeks, she worriedly said I wasn't showing as much as I should and urged me to eat more, as though I were her own sister.

"I can't carry heavy things either, can I?" I asked.

She said that was the most basic of the basics.

The bus soon pulled up at the stop by Seoyeong's apartment. I said goodbye to the woman and her baby and got off the bus. I walked up the long hill and turned onto Seoyeong's street. The lights were out at Bokhee's Kitchen, and an old woman was coming out of the restaurant with an electric rice cooker. I recognized the woman: she was the one who Bokhee helped out with cigarettes and side dishes. Her cart was parked out front and already loaded with a messy pile of pots, pans, and assorted plates and bowls. It was clearly a crime to steal someone's possessions when they were sick, even if they were friends. I hurried to confront the old woman when, all of a sudden, the sound of her voice calling Bokhee—*Bokhee!*—came to mind. Bokhee had gotten up to greet the old woman when she had called her by that name.

Why did the old woman call her "Bokhee" and not "Yeonhee"? Was she "Bokhee" to everyone who knew her? If I had asked her what her name was, would she have told me it was "Bokhee"? I wanted to know, but there was no way to find out unless she woke up. In the meantime, the old woman had left Bokhee's Kitchen with her cart, and the sound of the plates clacking together had grown faint in the distance.

I didn't feel like going after the old woman. Bokhee had just a month or two left, and her younger sister didn't seem like she deserved any inheritance. Besides, the old kitchenware was unlikely to make the list of bequests.

I went inside Bokhee's Kitchen and opened the frosted glass door at the back. The moment I opened the door, Bokhee's cell phone began to ring. The phone rang and rang, but I couldn't just answer it. If the caller asked who I was, I didn't have an adequate answer, and trying to explain the state Bokhee was in would be exhausting. I ignored the phone and went around the room with a bag, collecting Bokhee's underwear and towels, toothpaste, toothbrush, and soap from the bathroom. I knew she would not be needing underwear and towels and that the toiletries would not be used in the end, but still I tried to think of other things Bokhee would need. When the bag was almost full, I moved to leave the room but the phone started ringing again. I looked down at the phone, wondering who could be so keen on reaching Bokhee at this hour.

## 11

In the hospital hall with nearly all the lights off, the vending machine glowed softly like a satellite. Seoyeong went over to the vending machine, disturbing the pool of light; the sound of coins dropping into the slot was louder than usual. She returned with a paper cup of coffee. When she passed it to me, I sat up straight from leaning back against the wall and drank the coffee one sip at a time then tried to suppress a cough. It was the first cup of coffee I'd had in a long time. The sound of Seoyeong and me sipping our coffee echoed down to the far end of the hall.

Seoyeong had just finished recounting in careful detail the events of the past five days. She began by telling me how, through her college friend's brother, she had obtained the railway company's internal contact list, which included the contact information of many of the retired train conductors.

Seoyeong had high hopes, but when she finally got her hands on the contact list, Jung Woosik wasn't on it. She was disappointed, but quickly regrouped by making a list of all the train conductors who were over the age of sixty and reached out to them. It wasn't easy. Most of the numbers were wrong or no longer in service, and even when she was able to get in touch with one of them, she hadn't known where to begin. *Would you happen to know a train conductor named Jung Woosik? Do you know anything about a little girl who was found on the tracks at Cheongnyangni Station in 1983? Does the name Jung Munju ring a bell?* All Seoyeong could do was tell them briefly about the documentary she was making and ask these prepared questions, but the answers she received were for the most part vague and unfriendly. Some were disgruntled at being asked these questions when they had long retired; others wanted to know how she'd gotten their contact info. After each phone call, Seoyeong had to blast some music to wash the residual discomfort off of her.

*Time to give up?* she wondered.

Each time the thought occurred to her, she told me, her mind went to the actor who'd flown all the way from France to Korea for this film, and the determination on her face when she fearlessly went down onto the tracks and held up the cardboard sign. Seoyeong couldn't give up. Or rather, she didn't want to. When she was completely worn out after dozens of attempts, she finally connected with a former train conductor who said that he knew Jung Woosik well. She nearly screamed for joy.

His name was Choi Changnyong, and he was a long-time colleague of Jung Woosik's. He remembered the day Mr. Jung found the girl on the tracks. It was around 1983, when Mr. Jung was a novice train conductor, that he had brought a crying young girl into the night-shift room. She was small and very skinny. Mr. Jung had to hop back on another train, so the other train conductors tried giving snacks and toys to the girl to get her to stop crying.

"I remember it clear as day," he had slowly confirmed.

Seoyeong had clutched her phone with both hands and thanked him over and over through tears. She said she was grateful to Mr. Choi for not forgetting that day, and also to Jung Woosik for saving a life.

"Then, may I have Mr. Jung's contact information?" Seoyeong had asked cautiously once she had calmed somewhat.

There was silence. Seoyeong had felt her heart would explode.

—

Mr. Choi said that Jung Woosik had passed away five years earlier from illness. The moment I heard this, I felt a brutal chill that defied the summer heat. My shoulders rolled in and fits of cough burst out of my chest. I needed a proxy to act out this loneliness on my behalf. I imagined an actor turning into an ice statue in the middle of summer and tried to project my loneliness onto her, but this time the transference did not work. Habit had a way of not kicking in when you needed it. I leaned my head against the wall, waiting for this phantom cold that had pierced my reality to pass. That was when Seoyeong returned with the vending machine coffee. The warm drink could not drive the cold away, not the kind of cold that originated from deep within my heart.

I was already halfway through the cup of coffee when I saw Seoyeong's worried face. She said she'd gotten Mr. Jung's columbarium address from Mr. Choi, that I could go whenever I felt ready and that she would come with me. I managed a smile.

After a while, Seoyeong said that she'd despaired at the unexpected news, but that she was still half worried and half hopeful when she asked Mr. Choi this question: "Did you know that Mr. Jung named the girl he found at the tracks 'Munju'?"

Mr. Choi said he was fuzzy on the name, it was so long ago. But he did know that Mr. Jung had looked after her for almost a year. He remembered hearing happy anecdotes and stories about the girl growing up, and he was mostly glad to hear it but sometimes felt concerned. According to Mr. Choi, at the time Mr. Jung was engaged to a woman who would later become his wife. A thirty-year-old bachelor of marrying age bringing home a strange orphan did not sit well with his mother, future wife, or future in-laws. Mr. Choi had also broached the subject of sending the girl to a professional facility before tying the knot.

I'd had no idea that Mr. Jung was soon to be married. But then again, I wasn't old enough to pick up on adults' plans or understand what they meant. But I did belatedly wonder: Was he planning to formally adopt me when he was married and settled, the way Sister Gemma had assumed? Had he imagined his future children and me growing up like siblings? Maybe. The name "Jung Munju" was proof of such an intention.

Still . . .

Still, these were all maybes. He had walked off the screen where my life was being projected and never re-entered the scene, and, as of five years ago, he'd left the screen of this life altogether, so there was no evidence anywhere of what he had meant to do.

Forever.

"Anyway, this much I can guarantee," Mr. Choi had continued in a rather confident tone, "ever since Woosik confirmed that there were no missing-child reports at the Cheongnyangni Station—when it became clear that the parents were not looking for this girl—he put a lot of care into choosing an orphanage. On his days off, he would secretly scope out orphanages with good reputations, not just the ones assigned by the police station. At that time, there were many illegal orphanages that abused children. It would come up in the news every now and then. Woosik did what he could to avoid those horrible places."

Seoyeong was somewhat comforted by that.

Seoyeong later explained her film to Mr. Choi again and said she would like to interview and maybe film a scene with him if that was okay. Mr. Choi said that he was retired and running a small orchard in the country, so he was too busy to spare even a day. But he offered the number of Mr. Jung's wife, whom he thought she'd best talk to instead.

Seoyeong got off the phone with Mr. Choi and called Mr. Jung's wife's number right away. Mrs. Jung was nervous about being filmed and adamantly refused, but her eldest daughter, who happened to be there, showed interest. They made an appointment for a shoot the next day at 10 a.m., at the coffee shop in Hapjeong where Seoyeong worked.

"It's like . . . you know, the folded part of the photograph. Until you unfold it, you can't see that it was an important part of the full shot. Meeting her tomorrow could be something like that."

When Seoyeong ended her long story, I nodded and nodded as if it were the only thing I knew how to do.

Seoyeong and I got off the bench and walked side by side to the elevators. In the elevator, she said she was very surprised to hear that I had been going to the hospital to sit by the old woman from Bokhee's Kitchen. I could understand her surprise; Seoyeong had a tepid relationship with Bokhee even though they had been neighbors for a long time. While I gave Seoyeong a brief history of my relationship with Bokhee, the elevator arrived in the lobby.

"In my opinion, if eating at her restaurant three times is the entire extent of your relationship, you don't owe it to her to sit by her bedside. Coming by every now and then would be enough." Seoyeong sounded disapproving. I could understand why it was difficult for her to comprehend my decision to keep vigil by Bokhee's bedside every night, closely monitoring her condition and breathing. I occasionally had trouble understanding it myself.

When the elevator doors opened to the ground floor, Seoyeong cocked her head to the side and said, "By the way, the old lady's name isn't Bokhee, is it? I saw another name by the hospital room door."

"I think it's strange, too," I said. "Her real name is Chu

Yeonhee, so why did the neighborhood lady call her Bokhee? Besides, the restaurant is also named after 'Bokhee.'"

"Maybe it's her daughter's name."

"Daughter?"

"It's common practice in Korea to name your business after yourself or your child. My mother's generation often referred to women by their children's name. When I was young, the neighbors would call my mother 'Seoyeong.' 'Come look at this, Seoyeong.' 'Where are you off to, Seoyeong?' Something like that," she explained like it was a boring tidbit. She didn't notice the look of amazement on my face as she walked ahead of me across the lobby.

After Seoyeong left, I sat in front of the large-screen TV in the hospital lobby for a long time. I thought of the child in the photograph. Was Bokhee lying? Had she lied, telling everyone that the child was not her own because she was ashamed of having sent her own daughter away to Belgium? If so, was her daughter, like me, forced into the adoption process, sitting like baggage on a conveyor belt until the prospective parents chose us? There was one clue: the physical appearance of the child in the photo. I knew that very few people in Korea had her appearance and that it would be hard for someone who looked like her to be accepted in Korean society. Bokhee's reason for putting her up for adoption may have been that she could not handle raising a kid who would constantly face extreme social prejudice.

Scenes I did not want to see came to the forefront of my mind: the child in the photo at an international airport somewhere in Belgium, overwhelmed by apprehension and looking around wide-eyed; then, later, waking up from a nightmare to find herself in a strange house and being reminded—even in the most unreservedly happy moments of her life—of the fear and pain of abandonment. I could go on and on. Come to think of it, Bokhee had said that she was both grateful and sorry to the "number one" child who looked like me. I was familiar with that sentiment. "Grateful and sorry" was the "number one" excuse of parents who gave up their children.

The news came on the TV. The anchor's mid-to-low tone sounded as strange as a foreign language, and the torrent of jargon was especially incomprehensible today. But then again, Korean was a foreign language to me. I was clearly in a foreign country. *My mother's home,* I laughed. This country and the people of this country had abandoned me, and I had lived more than eighty percent of my life in France. *People like Bokhee,* I said to myself bitterly. *People like Bokhee, people like my mother, people who ran off instead of protecting and raising me, were no better than the orphanage director and the adoption agency that sold us for a commission. All of them were the same, a country crawling with people like that. That's what this country is. So why, why?*

Why did I come here? Why . . . here . . . ?

I leaned forward and hung my head. I stared at the floor, then quickly rose to my feet and staggered across the lobby, got into the elevator, got off the elevator and walked down the hall. When I got to Bokhee's room, I threw the door open and strode up to her bed without turning on the lights.

"Why did you abandon her, the real Bokhee?"

My voice sounded shrill even to my ears, but Bokhee continued to breathe peacefully, in and out, as though she were sound asleep. She looked like she would wake up and look at me with a blank expression if I were to grab her by the shoulders and shake her. *You didn't abandon her, you meant to get her back soon but it was too late. Tell me that's what happened,* I might have shrieked, half mad, if she had woken up.

I picked up my bag and rushed out of the room. I couldn't find it in me to spend the night at the hospital out of the goodness of my heart, a goodness that might never spring from my heart again.

I marched home from the hospital. The air was smothered by the heat of the day and stood still into the night, unable to push aside even a single strand of my hair. But I stumbled as if I were walking through a wild storm. After about thirty minutes of marching nonstop, I was in front of Bokhee's Kitchen. The lights were on inside and a familiar cart was parked out front. Inside the restaurant, the old woman had taken over a table and was drinking soju as if she were Bokhee.

I opened the door and went inside. The old woman didn't even look in my direction when she said, "It's closed. Get out." I ignored her and sat down in the chair across from her. Only then did she look up and snap, "Why are you sitting down? I said it's closed."

"What gives you the right to be here? I saw you the other day stealing the rice cooker and the plates." I couldn't care less about the rice cooker and the plates, and had no intention of picking a fight with the old woman, but my voice came out harsh.

"Steal? How is it stealing if I'm taking what's mine?"

"What's yours?"

"Bokhee made me a deal. If something were to happen to her, she said to take everything from the restaurant and sell it all. You hear me? She gave me ownership of everything in here. Everything's mine!"

"Bokhee? The woman who runs this restaurant is Bokhee? No, she's not Bokhee. She's Chu Yeonhee."

"What?"

"Let me tell you who Bokhee really is. The daughter she sent away to Belgium. The one she abandoned and forgot about. And here she would sit in a restaurant she named after her, pretending to wait for her with that sad look on her face. Am I right?"

The old woman gazed at me without a word. Silence hung in the air between us as we exchanged confused looks. After some time, she got up, returned with a fresh soju glass, and poured me one.

"Bokhee, the old bag of this restaurant, had a child and gave it up for adoption. Is that what you're telling me?" she asked in a gentler tone. "I don't know where you heard that, but Bokhee has no children. As far as I know."

When I asked her if she was absolutely sure, the old woman leaned in toward me as though she'd heard something intriguing and repeated, "'Absolutely sure'? 'Absolutely'? You're asking like some judge. Sure, I did hear something like that. When Bokhee was twenty-two or twenty-three, she got married and had a daughter right away who died before her first birthday. After that, she tried everything but couldn't get pregnant, so her husband and in-laws threw her out. Hey, listen . . ." She paused for a moment and continued, "This was fifty years ago. After fifty years, you can't remember what you did with which idiot. I drank myself into a stupor and fell asleep by a breezy little spot on a nice river, and when I woke up the world told me I was an old hag. So it's one or the other: drink until you wake up from the dream, or fall into a deep sleep you'll never wake up from."

The old woman had a surprising gift of the gab. What kind of person was she? Or rather, what kind of life had she led? I began to wonder about her. What name did she go by?

"A child," she said after throwing back two shots in a row. "A child was under her care once. It was someone else's kid. You know this story, don't you, Third Floor?"

"Was that someone else called Boksun?"

"Listen here. Do I look like the kind of person who cares what anyone's called? What's a name? Who cares if you're called Dogshit or Gold-buddha? Shit."

"You know about me, don't you?"

"You're the one on the third floor. That's why I call you 'Third Floor.' Isn't that right? No?"

"What else? What else do you know?"

"I know Bokhee's changed. At first I thought, *Why open up a restaurant only to sit on your bum in there all day?* She didn't care if there were customers, and she was living off her savings. But ever since you arrived, she came to life. You can't fool my eyes. You can fool a ghost, but not me."

The old woman twisted her mouth and laughed. It sounded like a laugh. I heard laughter, but her face betrayed anger or physical pain. It may have been her deep wrinkles and missing teeth, or that the muscles on her face had forgotten how to smile after all this time. She sat in silence for some time, then glared into space. After knocking back the remaining soju, she got up, pushing the chair back behind her. I asked the old woman, who was leaving without saying goodbye, why she hadn't gone to see Bokhee at the hospital.

"What for? She can't recognize people anyway," she answered. "Listen, I earn a day to live a day. If I don't earn today, I starve the next day. That is my life. Dying isn't sad. Living, being alive is what's shitty."

When I didn't respond, she added, "Just let me know when she passes," and left.

The old woman had resolved one misunderstanding, but she hadn't shared everything she knew about Bokhee. I knew there was more. I had seen the old woman tense up when I mentioned Boksun. Bokhee, Yeonhee, and Boksun. In order to get a closer look at the lives behind these names, I would have to speak with the old woman again. And as soon as I reached this conclusion, I realized I'd forgotten to ask what those names meant. Misun, Hyeonsuk, Jeongmi, Yeongok, Jahye, Geumsun, Nanhee . . . I listed the names that might go with the old woman and gazed down at the soju glass in front of me the way Bokhee used to.

Behind me, the cell phone rang, playing a melody that I now had memorized. I slowly turned around. I got up off the chair, opened the frosted glass door, and went into Bokhee's room, making a bet with myself, which I lost in the end: the phone did not stop ringing before my hand reached it.

Holding my breath, I answered the phone.

# 12

Train conductor Jung Woosik got married in the winter of 1983, immediately after he sent me to the Nazareth Orphanage, and had a daughter and son two years apart. He had built himself a lovely home and family. His mother, the very one who'd made me susubukkumi, never got over the death of her son and now lived a reclusive life in Yeongwol, Gangwondo. "Yeongwol" meant "smooth crossing," an ironic name for a place with many high peaks and rapids, according to the dictionary.

"So I haven't told Granny about Munju-unnie yet. She rarely picks up the phone and when she does, she's too hard of hearing to understand me. The best way to communicate with her is to go see her in person, but I have to clear my schedule for a whole day to go down there."

Sitting across the table from me was the daughter of Jung Woosik, explaining where her grandmother was. The important information she was relaying did not interest me as much as the fact that she was calling me "Munju-unnie"—sister. It was a designation that hit me in the heart without leaving a mark. Her name was Mungyeong, and she was an English instructor in her early thirties. I think Hwigyeong was the younger brother's name. Munju, Mungyeong, Hwigyeong. I was becoming accustomed to this naming pattern of repeating one syllable.

"'Mun' as in 'pattern' and 'gyeong' as in 'sunlight.' I guess if it had to mean something, it would be 'pattern of sunlight.' My brother's 'hwi' means 'shining,' so that'll be 'shining sunlight.' And yes, Father named us both."

Seoyeong's camera closed in on Mungyeong, while she carefully explained the meaning of the names. My eyes were naturally drawn to Mungyeong's face as well. Mungyeong—the name was not a metaphor. I could not look away from the glowing face that must have inherited the train conductor's features.

I asked cautiously, "So there's a good possibility that the 'mun' in my name also means 'pattern.' Did your father ever mention it when he was alive?"

"Well, I'm not sure . . ."

"I guess he never . . . told you about me."

Mungyeong must have picked up on my disappointment. She shook her head and asserted that wasn't true.

"Since I was young, I heard Granny and Dad talk about you all the time. But they always referred to you as aga, not by your name. I only just found out that this aga had a name that was similar to mine."

"Aga?"

"Yes, they always called you aga—baby. 'This was aga's favorite. I hope she found good parents. She must be married by now.' Something like that."

I laughed. Mungyeong laughed along as though embarrassed. As I laughed, I thought about the bad and good things that came of meeting Mungyeong. The train conductor had had no intention of adopting me, but had remembered me. Both the good and the bad elicited the same numb response in me.

I wanted to be numb.

"My summer vacation is coming up in two weeks, and I was going to visit Granny. I will definitely ask her how they came up with the name Munju."

I said I looked forward to hearing from her. Knowing I would soon visit the house where my senses and memories began, I felt an emptiness I couldn't explain. I imagined it was like the sudden letdown a runner feels when they finally reach the finish line after going full speed for the entire race.

"Susubukkumi," I said, breaking a short silence.

"Huh?"

"Susubukkumi. Your grandmother made me that on rainy days. You have that too?"

"Oh, yes. Tons."

"When you see her, could you let her know that I miss her cooking very much? And if by any chance she remembers anything about what I was wearing or any objects I had on me when I was found at the train tracks, I would love to know. Also . . ." I paused and took a deep breath. Mungyeong was gazing back at me across the table. "Also that I am alive today partly because she fed me, that I got on a plane and came here even though I'm pregnant because I missed the taste of her cooking. Please tell her that as well."

Mungyeong blinked her large eyes, and Seoyeong and Eun looked at each other, their mouths hanging open. Seoyeong seemed the most shocked of them all. Mungyeong smiled from ear to ear and congratulated me, and Eun quickly regained his composure, but Seoyeong continued to look at me with bewilderment.

"Cut," Seoyeong said, her voice trembling.

After filming, Mungyeong cautiously came up to me as though she had been waiting to say something off-camera.

"Uh, would it be all right if I gave you a hug?" I didn't know what to say. Mungyeong continued, "Whenever I traveled someplace far away, Dad would always hug me when I returned. And I came here in his place today."

"Well . . . okay," I replied.

Mungyeong smiled, opened her arms, and hugged me. Her breath was as sweet as sugar, the palms of her hands soft as she patted me on the back, and her voice rang gently in my ear as she said, "Thank you for coming back to look for Dad." I had finally found traces of the train conductor in Mungyeong.

With Mungyeong's arms wrapped around me, I sobbed.

After Mungyeong left, Soyul and Eun talked about dining options in the area while Seoyeong, looking like she was dying to talk, hung around me. I knew that eating together after a shoot was a rule, but I had someplace to be. I told Seoyeong that I couldn't join them, and Seoyeong looked ready to burst into tears.

"Are you going to look after the old woman from the restaurant?" she asked.

"I have to make a stop before that. Is something wrong?"

"Hospitals are full of germs."

Seoyeong's eyes turned red, prompting Eun to chide her by reminding her that many pregnant women worked at the hospital and that she had nothing to worry about. I grabbed Seoyeong's hands and assured her I would be okay and that I wanted to do this, and Seoyeong slowly nodded with her eyes on my stomach.

I grabbed my bag and left the coffee shop. I got a cab right away and headed to the Children's Services office in Seongbuk, where a letter Bokhee had waited ten years to receive had finally arrived. I'd heard about the letter the previous night.

When I was in Bokhee's room the night before, I picked up the ringing phone and was greeted with the voice of a young man who was going off on a rant. "I called you dozens of times over several days. I thought nighttime might be better for you so I called after work, too, every chance I got. I'm going to bill you for the late hours," and on and on, alternating between making fun of Bokhee and worrying about her. He sounded like a friend.

I finally managed to get a word in. "Excuse me, I've answered the phone on Bokhee's behalf . . ."

The man demanded to know who I was. As I was telling him about Bokhee, he let out many heavy sighs and asked for the name of the hospital and the doctor's prognosis.

Then, he began a very long story.

He identified himself as a clerk at Children's Services who had become acquainted with "Ms. Chu Yeonhee," as he called her, about four years ago. I could tell that this was the man from Children's Services to whom Seoyeong had given directions to Bokhee's Kitchen. For the past ten years, Ms. Chu had been coming by Children's Services every month asking them to mail a letter, all to Baek Bokhee, who had been adopted to Belgium. It was against the rules for Children's Services to give out the contact information of adoptive parents to biological or foster parents without consent, which left Ms. Chu with no choice but to send the letters through Children's Services. She was famous among the staff there. Sending letters so consistently without any reply was rare, or rather, unique. Besides, Ms. Chu wasn't even Baek Bokhee's biological mother. On paper, Baek Bokhee's biological mother was Baek Boksun, and Chu Yeonhee was only a foster parent.

Most of the letters sent over the years were returned, and even when the letters weren't returned, not once did anyone write back. The letters may have been returned because Baek Bokhee's address had changed, but there was also the possibility that her adoptive parents were keeping them from her. One way or another, Children's Services had no way of knowing. The only address and phone number they had on file was unconfirmed; the information they'd found on documents long ago was never updated in the system.

Incredibly, a letter had arrived from Baek Bokhee for the very first time. No one at Children's Services dared open it. This letter was Chu Yeonhee's to receive and read first.

"It's heartbreaking. Just when a letter has finally come . . ."

The clerk let out another heavy sigh. I asked him if I could pick up the letter on her behalf. The man thought it over, then finally agreed to give me the letter, but only on one condition—that I email him a photo or video proof of me reading the letter to Bokhee. I agreed to his request. Even without prompting, I would have done whatever I could to give him proof that Bokhee had received the letter.

The cab pulled up in front of Children's Services.

I took out my cell phone, called the clerk, and waited impatiently for him.

# 13

*Dear Yeonhee:*

*Hello, Yeonhee.*

*How are you? Are you in good health?*

*I am quite at a loss now as I write this letter, having woken up in the middle of the night. I am not accustomed to expressing my feelings and thoughts in words, and writing in English and not French makes it much, much harder. I'm writing in English because I forgot all my Korean and as I remember, you spoke a little English. The neighborhood . . . I remember a mix of Korean and English coming from everywhere. You don't still live there, do you?*

*I left Korea in 1987, so it's been over thirty years already. In the years it took for me to become forty you must've turned seventy. How can I fit thirty years' worth of history in one letter? It's impossible. It's impossible, but I will tell you as much as I can, as honestly as I can.*

*Yeonhee, let me begin with the parts that I am sure you will not want to hear: in Belgium, I was not happy. Like most children like me, I always felt lost in my adoptive family and was not able to receive the affection I deserved. I spent my whole childhood confused about who I was, and I am still confused from time to time. Adoption saved me from abandonment, but at the same time, it robbed me of the most important part of myself. The more miserable I was in Belgium, the more I resented you. Maybe it was harder to forgive you because I remembered the love I received from you. I still remember it quite vividly. The day you took me to Children's Services, there was a formal meeting with my adoptive parents. The awkward atmosphere made me feel judged, even though everyone was smiling at me. The adoption process happened so fast after that, numerous documents, departure and arrival . . . I was so scared and lonely, but you ignored me for the entire process and didn't even come to the airport on the day I left Korea. Whatever your reasons for making that decision, I wasn't ready to hear them. And I could not fully trust the voice inside me that said I wanted or needed to see you.*

*To be honest, I haven't opened the letters you sent me over the last ten years. I picked them up from my adoptive parents' place every time I went to visit, but I put them in an old box and forgot about them. When my adoptive parents moved a few years ago, I no longer received your letters, which once came to me as naturally as water flowing downhill.*

*Just recently, I've begun to take the forgotten letters out of the old box to read, one at a time.*

*Three months ago during a routine exam, a tumor was found on my left breast. The doctor who examined the sonogram suggested a biopsy, the result of which would come in one month. That month was a test of patience. It was during this month, when time seemed to have stopped, that I started to read your letters. I had to.*

*Strangely, the tumor reminded me that I'd been lucky enough to have you take me in and look after me—that is, my life was extended thanks to your affection and work. You were a woman in your thirties who was remarkably devoted to nursing my mother and raising me, and I never forgot that.*

*Reading one of your letters took hours of flipping through the dictionary and translating sentences, which soon became a relaxing exercise that calmed my fears. When your letters began to run out, I felt I would like to express my gratitude to you regardless of the biopsy result, and I was sure I couldn't ignore or put off this wish any longer.*

*Yeonhee, I hope this belated reply makes you glad.*

*It's been a long time coming, but I can finally say that I want to meet you. I want to meet you and learn more about my life. I don't know what else to say, but I mean this sincerely.*

*P.S. If I come to Korea, with your understanding and permission I would like to visit Mother's grave with you. I remember holding your hand and visiting there several times. You must remember where it is? I'd like to show Mother who I grew up to be.*

*This is my mobile number.*

"Should I stop filming now?" came the voice of the young nurse. I nodded, and the nurse handed back my cell phone. The phone now contained a video of me reading Baek Bokhee's letter translated into Korean for Bokhee—or rather, Yeonhee, to everyone including me, now that the real Bokhee had appeared.

The nurse mumbled to herself as she massaged Yeonhee's arms and legs, "Granny's a good person. A good person's got to live longer. Get well and wake up, Granny."

I silently gazed over at the nurse before leaving Yeonhee's hospital room with her urine bag. I made my way down the hall as slowly as I could, emptied the bag in the toilet, and returned to find the nurse had gone and in her place was a shared hospital-appointed caretaker. Standing a few steps back, I watched the caretaker change Yeonhee out of her hospital clothes, put on a fresh diaper, and use a washcloth to clean her face, down to the neck, the loose folds of skin on her chest and stomach, and her privates. Looking at another person's naked body made me uneasy, but knowing that this body was the final destination I too would arrive at one day somehow made it bearable.

When the caretaker left, I took Yeonhee's hand in mine. Yeonhee had indeed put a child she had raised like her own up for adoption, but I couldn't hate her for it. Not knowing what else to do, I squeezed Yeonhee's hand harder. The liver spots and bony knuckles indicated this was the hand of an old person, but the hand was so small. "Small," I whispered. I couldn't believe that she had toiled for decades with these small hands. I couldn't believe these hands raised Baek Bokhee, looked after Baek Boksun, and cooked for me. I took her hands, nails neglected and grown long, and carefully placed them under the covers.

I would leave the hospital and call the number on Baek Bokhee's letter. I would tell her about Yeonhee's condition, and that there was no way to find Baek Boksun's grave at this time. I wanted to delay being the bearer of unwelcome news, like putting off a school assignment.

Grave . . .

"Grave," I said to myself, bringing to mind a sentence from Baek Bokhee's letter. She'd been led by the hand to her mother's grave many times, so the grave was likely located someplace close to where they had lived. To find Baek Boksun's grave, I had to first find the location of the house where Yeonhee had raised Bokhee with Baek Boksun. There was only person who might have that information. I picked up my bag and rushed back to Bokhee's Kitchen with no plan but to simply sit in front of the restaurant and wait for her.

# 14

"She just left Itaewon without so much as a goodbye, and I didn't hear from her for twenty years. I heard she worked at a public clinic in Cheonan. Spent years at a convalescent home near Gunsan that you could only get to by boat. Then she came crawling back here and opened a restaurant. The woman who couldn't make a decent soup, now all old and wrinkled. It makes me laugh."

The old woman really laughed. It was the first time I saw what her face looked like when she smiled. No twisted mouth or twitching muscles, but a bright-eyed childlike face with high cheekbones. I had never seen that face before.

The old woman was unleashing a barrage of information she had on Yeonhee. Hometown, how the conditions of her life changed during the war, the sorrow of losing her younger brother and daughter . . . She hadn't even gotten to Baek Boksun and Bokhee yet, but I was surprised to see her open up, given that up to this point she'd been invariably indifferent or hostile. Only after the fact, only after I realized that Yeonhee was a much lonelier person than I had assumed, did I come to understand what the old woman had done that night. To the old woman, I was one of the very few people on earth who would remember Yeonhee when she was gone. Someone to remember Yeonhee's life and mourn her death—the person one most desperately needed when facing the end.

I waited for the old woman to finish a chapter of her story, then cautiously broached the subject as I poured her a fresh glass of soju. "You've heard of Baek Bokhee, right? The Bokhee of 'Bokhee's Kitchen.' Yeonhee has been waiting to hear from her for a long time."

I wasn't sure if she would react as defensively as she had when I brought up Baek Boksun. The old woman glanced at me, a cloudy light glinting in her eyes. Cloudy and cloudier still was a look I could gaze at forever and never figure out.

"I found Baek Bokhee's phone number and spoke with her today," I said. "She's coming to Seoul in two weeks. The thing is . . . Bokhee wants to visit her biological mother's grave. She said it was her wish to go. So . . . if you know where Baek Boksun's grave is, let me know. You must let me know. That's what Yeonhee would have wanted."

"Boksun or Boknam or whatever her name is, you think I know where she's buried?" the old woman spat.

When our eyes met, she emptied her glass and rubbed her eyes hard with her fists. "I gotta go. I'm tired."

She got up quickly and, even as she staggered drunk, dragged two chairs with her. These were today's ration of Yeonhee's bequest to her. Most of the tables and chairs at Bokhee's Kitchen were gone by now and many of the kitchen shelves were now bare. I fetched two pans from the kitchen, loaded them onto the old woman's cart, and tied down the chairs tight so they wouldn't fall off. The old woman stood at the head of the cart and watched me intently.

The old woman dragged the cart away from Bokhee's Kitchen, throwing a glance at me before turning the corner. For some reason I raised my arm and waved at her, while she stood and watched for a long time. She was a good distance away and it was dark, so I could not see the look on her face.

Having heard about Yeonhee's life from the old woman, there were many things I could imagine about her now. The oldest scene I could picture was this: Sirens blaring while the streets filled with people pouring out of their houses in terror. The cries of children and livestock, the acrid smell of bombs everywhere, the roars and clanks of tanks and bombers, anxiety in the air and the omens of death advancing fast . . . These were the things that dominated Seoul the year Yeonhee was four years old, Korean age. In the midst of war, with people dying and bodies rotting on the ground, Yeonhee's mother gave birth to a son. The baby was born safely and there were capable adults who could protect the child, but the protective shell around the children was unsound. Yeonhee's father had left Seoul immediately after he saw his newborn son in order to avoid the draft. He never returned to his family again, and the ceasefire did not come as quickly as everyone had expected. Yeonhee's younger brother perished only three months after his birth. He was likely malnourished and died from a not very fatal disease. When Yeonhee's brother passed away, she was just a child, too young to know the difference between dying and falling asleep. She would have watched sadly as her mother held her brother's body in her arms and wailed until her voice gave out, but she would not have known the meaning of the gesture.

After three years the Korean War ended, and Yeonhee's mother remarried. She would have been thoroughly dismayed by her first marriage, which had culminated in her husband's abandonment and the death of her son, and would have wanted to get as far away from those memories as possible. Yeonhee grew up as a spare in the new household her mother married into, and watched while her mother had two children and raised them with a new man. That Yeonhee was an unloved outlier in this family was easy enough to deduce based on the behavior of her guardian and insurance beneficiary, her younger half-sister.

Yeonhee was finally able to get away from her mother when she came of age. She worked during the day and attended nursing college at night, her career choice likely driven by her wish to be financially independent as soon as possible. Maybe her reason for getting married not long after she became a nurse had something to do with that too. I heard from the old woman what had happened to Yeonhee after she married: she was married when she was twenty-two or twenty-three, and when her daughter died after her first birthday and Yeonhee couldn't get pregnant again, her husband and in-laws drove her out. . . .

Coming out of Bokhee's Kitchen and climbing the steps to the third floor, I found myself unable to ignore that scene anymore. In my imagination, Yeonhee's face was uncannily calm and cold as she held her daughter's body in her arms. What other expression could emerge on the face of someone who had lost all hope and will at once? As she felt her daughter's blood turn cold and her muscles stiffen, she would have thought of the agony of losing her younger brother, and would have lost the will to forge on through a life that kept snatching people away from her without mercy. The crushing sense of defeat that she would have to endure for a long time after . . .

I was convinced that before she met Boksun and Bokhee, Yeonhee would have lived through a period that was similar to my college years. Born into the world without knowing why and living against my will, my time during college culminated in a period of blackout when I was fundamentally always gravitating toward death. That would have been why Yeonhee did not turn a blind eye to the ailing Boksun and her child Bokhee. She would not have been able to if she tried, as the mother and daughter would have reminded Yeonhee of the two lives she hadn't been able to protect, and she would never, ever let another life, no matter whose, expire and turn cold in her arms. A life was solace and salvation for Yeonhee.

Chu Yeonhee had come to mean more to me now than just an old woman who worked at Bokhee's Kitchen. She was a woman who continued to dream through all her losses, who was wounded but tried hard not to let others suffer from the same wounds—she was a singular woman.

Chu Yeonhee, born 1948, second mother to Baek Bokhee.

The next day, I received a call from Children's Services. Until that phone call, I was not aware that while Baek Bokhee was also an adoptee, her situation was different from mine. There was only two years' difference between us and we were adopted overseas around the same time, but she knew exactly who gave birth to her and raised her, and this information was on the record. Baek Bokhee had the document that I did not have: the birth record.

I got off the phone and visited the Children's Services office, where the clerk gave me a copy of her birth records. Only the family or relatives of the adoptee had access to this document, but the clerk made an exception given Yeonhee and Bokhee's situation, and allowed me, a third party, to have a copy. He had called me that morning to thank me for the video I had sent him, and told me he'd had no idea that Baek Bokhee was coming to Korea soon and that she wanted to visit her mother's grave. He expressed doubt when I said her grave must be somewhere in Itaewon, but encouraged me to come down to the Children's Services office and check Baek Bokhee's documents, where I would find her last address in Korea. I could glean from his kind offer that he wanted to give Baek Bokhee the opportunity to visit her mother's grave.

In an empty conference room at Children's Services, I slowly looked over Baek Bokhee's birth records. The documents contained the history of how Baek Bokhee was born and raised up to that point—how Yeonhee was a nurse at the public clinic when she met pregnant Baek Boksun, and how Yeonhee came to be involved in Baek Boksun's childbirth and raising Baek Bokhee—in addition to the basic information on Baek Bokhee. According to the records,

Baek Boksun was eighteen when she became pregnant with Bokhee, while Yeonhee was thirty at the time. Baek Boksun's cause of death and funerary process were not specified, nor was there any information on Bokhee's biological father—name, age, or other information to help identify him—apart from his occupation. The reason for relinquishing custody of the child, the information I was most curious about, was simply "change of circumstances" and "at the advice of friends and relations," a standard answer that was clearly intended to conceal the truth. The signature on the bottom of the birth record, *Chu Yeonhee*, confirmed that the information had been recorded by Yeonhee herself.

"She's no ordinary woman," said the clerk when he came into the conference room with something for me to drink. "It was hard to find someone as brave as Yeonhee back in those days."

I looked up from the birth record, puzzled by what he meant.

"What do you call it in English? Ah, yes. 'Military camp-town.' 'Town for soldiers.' According to the birth records, Baek Bokhee's biological father was an American soldier. Military camptowns today are just areas with bustling nightlife, but it was different in the 1970s. A single woman with a respectable job getting together with Baek Boksun, who worked at the military camptown, and forming a sort of alternative family together was entirely unheard of."

"Alternative family?"

"Not a traditional family of marriage and blood ties, but one that shares livelihood and home. A community that is in some ways more like a family than a traditional one. Yeonhee was the head of this family."

The clerk continued to explain what military camptowns were like in Baek Boksun's day, and by the time his story was over, I had to look over Baek Bokhee's birth record, as written by Yeonhee, once more.

After I left Children's Services, I headed to Hapjeong. Baek Bokhee was to arrive in ten days. I badly wanted to find the grave before she got here. But I couldn't go looking for Baek Boksun's grave on my own; there wasn't enough time.

When I got to Hapjeong and opened the coffee shop door, I saw Seoyeong behind the L-shaped bar, engrossed in making coffee. I had so much to tell her.

## 15

In the years following the Korean War, the US military continued to send soldiers overseas, and a town that provided things for the soldiers to eat, drink, and consume was established around the base camp. This was the military camptown, or gijichon, as it was called in Korean.

"But until the early 1990s, the word gijichon was taboo. Most Koreans never said that word; it was as though everyone had fallen under collective hypnosis. I only found out recently in articles I looked up for research that gijichon were covered up and concealed because of the sense of debasement Koreans felt in relation to a world power, in addition to the sexual depravity."

Seoyeong shared what she must have researched over the past two days. She had suggested that we find the neighborhood where Baek Boksun had worked and lived before she had Bokhee, so now we were walking along a street behind Itaewon Station.

After looking over Baek Bokhee's birth record at the coffee shop in Hapjeong, Seoyeong expressed her wish to help me find Baek Boksun's grave. She said she wanted to film the process and showed great resolve by saying that since this would be an unscheduled filming, she would film it alone without Eun and Soyul's help and edit it so that the scenes would fit naturally into the documentary. If we were successful, the latter part of the story would be about my search for Baek Boksun's grave. We had nothing to film before we heard back from Mungyeong anyway. If Mungyeong forgot about the favor I'd asked and we never got together again, Seoyeong's film would remain unfinished.

"The club where Baek Boksun worked and lived before she moved in with Yeonhee would have been somewhere around here," Seoyeong said.

I stopped and looked around. The street we had just passed was lined with a supermarket, Turkish restaurant, and currency exchange, and felt like a portal to a different time. It was almost as if we'd just come out of a long, dark tunnel. The gijichon lay before our eyes, starker than any place I had seen in Seoul.

Although it was only ten minutes from Itaewon Station, the old gijichon had been excluded from development over the past thirty years, Seoyeong said. The area by Itaewon Station was full of glamorous restaurants, franchise coffee shops, and people ready to spend money. But the old gijichon, once the biggest commercial area in Seoul, began to shrink in the 1990s, when the population of American soldiers declined and parts of the camp were moved to other cities. It now lay in ruins, a place time forgot.

The streets became even more dilapidated the further we went in. It reminded me of the slums on the outskirts of Paris, where immigrants or the undocumented lived. Shuttered stores, houses with windows ripped out, men in hats pulled down over their faces staggering around, women wearing flashy makeup and not enough clothes, graffiti splashed on the walls, piles of garbage on every corner—all unmistakable signs of a slum.

According to the clerk at Children's Services, up until the early 1990s, the women who worked here received protection from the government but remained strictly isolated. Most Koreans admitted that what these women did was necessary, but they were not respected. They were openly reviled and the mixed-race children they had were ill-treated and considered a disgrace. The clerk said that the public clinic where Yeonhee worked as a nurse was the very symbol of society's discrimination against the women who worked at gijichon. The physicians and nurses at the clinic were reluctant to touch the women's bodies, and when they came in for STD or pregnancy tests, all the medical tools were thoroughly disinfected after. If any of them were suspected of having contracted a disease from an American soldier, they were quarantined in a facility that was no different from a private jail and held there by the clinic staff.

At the workplace where this discrimination was routine, Yeonhee was able to befriend the very object of this discrimination and become her family. It would have taken no small courage for Yeonhee to not only help Baek Boksun deliver her baby, but go so far as to raise the child alongside her in Yeonhee's home. Probably as much courage is it took Henri and Lisa to take me, a person of a different color, into their family.

"Shall we take a break?" Seoyeong asked, glancing down worriedly at my belly. Wooju was at nineteen weeks, and the bump on my stomach was now large enough to draw attention. Seoyeong and I made our way into a narrow alley, put our bags down on some cement steps, and sat down. She passed her cell phone to me, saying she'd found some pictures on the Internet of this area thirty to forty years ago.

Store signs in English, women in miniskirts waving bottles of beer, two strapping American soldiers grabbing each other by the collar, and a woman smoking a cigarette with a look of someone who has momentarily forgotten her own existence . . . Pop music, the smell of cologne, someone's melancholy song . . . I could almost sense them coming out of the photograph.

The clerk at Children's Services had told me that women who worked here at the time had easy-to-pronounce English names like Jenny, Cassie, Ginny, or Nicki. Did Baek Boksun also go by Jenny or Cassie? Like so many Ginnys and Nickis, did she dream of marrying an American soldier and moving to the United States with him?

"I can't say for sure because I didn't live through those times, but the statistics I looked up indicate that such cases were rare. American soldiers did not usually consider marrying a gijichon woman. The high rate of single-mother births and adoptions supports this. It was much harder back then for a woman to raise a child alone than it is today. And if the child was mixed-race, their circumstances would have been especially harsh."

Listening to Seoyeong, I carefully studied each picture again. A whirl of breeze rolled by and tousled my hair. I noticed that the summer heat in Seoul had abated somewhat. The sunlight fell gently on the crown of my head instead of beating down, and the dark-green pigments weighing down the thick leaves on every tree had become visibly lighter. If Wooju did their duty as a fetus and developed nicely over the rest of the summer, through the coming autumn and early winter, I would be meeting them at the end of this year or early next year. The honest work of time was a relief and consolation to me.

At that moment, the sound of a baby's cry came from a house nearby. Was Baek Bokhee born in this neighborhood? I wondered. There was a good chance, but I couldn't know for sure. The birth record only had Baek Bokhee's date of birth and her address when she was adopted, not her place of birth, which meant that Baek Boksun could have given birth and recuperated at the public clinic or even at Yeonhee's house. The only thing I knew for certain was that Yeonhee "delivered" Bokhee. Taking Bokhee from between Baek Boksun's bloodied legs, Yeonhee had carefully held Bokhee as she washed off the blood and discharge with warm water and cut her umbilical cord.

When was the name "Bokhee" given to her?

Whose idea was it to take one syllable from "Boksun" and one from "Yeonhee?"

Now . . .

Now there was no one who knew that story.

Baek Bokhee was born in 1978, under the dictatorship, when poverty and hovels were commonplace. After "delivering" Bokhee, Yeonhee would have whispered through tears, "My god . . . children are born . . . even into worlds such as this one." When Yeonhee sat next to Boksun and put Bokhee, her umbilical cut not yet healed, in Boksun's arms, Boksun would have also looked at her daughter, overwhelmed by feelings she could not explain. That would have been the beginning of the family of two mothers and a daughter. I was sure that this community would have embodied beauty in its purest form. Bokhee was, as her name suggested, indeed "lucky and lucky," at least until she became acquainted with discrimination and sorrow. Or rather, Yeonhee and Boksun must have known from the moment Bokhee was born that Bokhee would face discrimination and sorrow for looking different from most Koreans. They were concerned and, as it turned out, exactly right about Bokhee's future.

"So the owner of Bokhee's Kitchen wasn't her foster mother, but a second mother. So why did she give away Bokhee after raising her as her own? The reason stated in the birth record can't be the whole story, can it?" Seoyeong asked as the baby's cries calmed.

"If Yeonhee had abandoned her for such a simple reason, she wouldn't have waited all this time to hear back from Bokhee."

"So then, was it for Baek Boksun?"

"Well," I replied, "the camera will give us a more truthful answer to that question."

Seoyeong looked down at the camera and back at me, and nodded in agreement.

Baek Boksun died four years after Baek Bokhee was born. She was only twenty-two. She wound up in a gijichon at seventeen, met Bokhee's biological father, and became a mother the following year. She became acquainted with the ways of the world too early and departed this life just as quickly, leaving behind Bokhee and countless unlived days. Yeonhee would have come home from Baek Boksun's funeral, looked down at Bokhee, who would have been sound asleep without a care in the world, and reaffirmed her vow to protect the child.

But it didn't last. There was little doubt that Yeonhee began to change her mind as Bokhee grew up. Yeonhee would have learned that it was impossible to offer Bokhee complete protection from the hostility of the world; there was only so much she could do. The option of adoption would have slowly corkscrewed its way into her vulnerable mind. Whereas the adoption process happened in a flash, and it was irreversible.

The life Yeonhee would have lived after she gave up Baek Bokhee and left Itaewon to live in Cheonan and the island near Gunsan—there was no one around to testify to those years. But I had no trouble picturing her coming home from work at a public clinic or convalescent home to turn the lights on to an empty house, her face emerging in the dark looking more exhausted than the day before, worn down by loneliness and incremental aging—the face of someone who cannot stop picking at the wounds in her heart. . . . Twenty years would have passed in this way.

And then one day, Yeonhee started over by returning to the neighborhood where she had lived with Bokhee and did something that had nothing to do with nursing: opened a restaurant. Maybe her wish was to see Bokhee just once more before she died. Bokhee's Kitchen—Yeonhee's workplace, home, and proof of existence—would have been a different kind of letter, carrying the hope of reunion. This was the one truth proving that Baek Bokhee was Yeonhee's daughter as well as Baek Boksun's, and that the life Bokhee had lived was not a lie.

Because Baek Bokhee was Chu Yeonhee's universe.

# 16

The night after Seoyeong and I visited the old gijichon, I became ill. I was running a fever and could hardly open my eyes from the oppressive fatigue. I had been pushing myself hard for the past few days. The stomach pain was what concerned me the most. It looked as if my stomach was protruding more than usual, and it felt more stiff in general. I went to bed early, but Seoyeong's mattress only worsened the pain in my back and legs.

Sleep did not come.

As time passed, my optimism that everything would turn out fine and that I would get through this grew thin. What really scared me, however, was the fear that Wooju's haven would collapse. "Stay close to me. Don't go anywhere. Don't leave me by myself, please . . ." I was murmuring to myself, arms wrapped around my stomach, when my phone rang. I sprung out of bed, crawled across the room to my bag, and held up the phone with both hands.

"Filming has been canceled for a whole week, and I was wondering how you were doing," said Soyul on the other end of the line. I clearly remembered Soyul saying that it was the duty of the director and staff to protect the actor, and that I should ask for help whenever I needed it.

Instead of asking Soyul how she was, I told her truthfully that I was unwell.

Soyul and Seoyeong each got in a cab and came to Itaewon. They examined my state, looked up obstetricians' offices with emergency rooms, then called a cab. During the cab ride, Seoyeong did not let go of my hand, and it was thanks to that support that I was able to battle my fears.

At the emergency room, I received an ultrasound right away. The doctor said I was experiencing temporary pain from putting my body through too much strain, and that plenty of rest should do it. I was moved to a hospital room where I would get the prescribed IV fluids and rest until morning. Soyul left because she had work in the morning, but Seoyeong stayed. I felt bad for Seoyeong. I felt bad, but I couldn't bring myself to tell her not to worry and go home.

I needed her.

"Can I ask you a question?" asked Seoyeong. She was lying under a blanket on a narrow cot; the lights in the ward were out and the hospital halls had grown quiet. I told her she didn't have to be so cautious with me, that of course she could ask me anything she wanted, and rolled over to face her.

"So what I want to know is . . ." Seoyeong paused for a moment. "Why you are sure that it was the railroad tracks? I was curious."

"Why am I sure?"

"Maybe you weren't abandoned on the tracks. Maybe you were wandering around Cheongnyangni Station and somehow ended up on the tracks. If you were three or four years old, you wouldn't have known that the tracks were dangerous. But if you insist that the place where you were abandoned was on the tracks and nowhere else . . . it's too heartbreaking for the little girl you were."

Silence flowed.

Unable to say anything, I rolled over on my back again and looked up at the ceiling.

The train tracks were where I was found. No one had seen me the moment I was abandoned, and the train conductor who found me was no longer in this world. Besides, I had no memory of that day or any day leading up to it, so where I had been before the train tracks was beyond my memory.

For a long time, all I could do was imagine it: walking along the tracks with my biological mother and losing grip of her hand at some point; the hazy silhouette of my biological mother running far away, leaving me at the tracks with my face streaked in tears; the sound of the train screeching to a sudden stop, and the train conductor's sigh of relief as he picked me up . . . I pictured it all from a distance like I was in the audience watching a play or film.

Seoyeong was right in pointing out that telling myself I was abandoned on the train tracks made me feel sorry for myself. But self-pity was a like dark pit on the surface of life: one could fall in by accident but no one could stay in it forever. There was a time when I had sunk into a self-pity that necessitated isolation, but I did not love being in that state. Not even for a second.

The train tracks could have been a conceptual space I had formed in order to hate my biological mother. This was not a simple hatred, but an entrenched one that precluded any chance of understanding and forgiveness. Placing her ignorant wrongdoing on the cold metal tracks meant that I would not have to carry the burden of forgiving her. Perhaps my life so far had been bolstered by my resentment toward her, and maybe I was afraid of sympathizing with her desperate situation and having to forgive her for abandoning me. Who would have thought that this realization would come to me in, of all places, the in-patient wing of an obstetrics clinic in Seoul? I wanted to find any clue that could reconstruct even just a piece of my biological mother, and yet I'd spent a portion of my life harboring unmitigated bitterness toward her.

Seoyeong must have been tired, because she fell asleep soon after and began to snore lightly. Seeing both of her legs sticking out from under the blanket, I reached out with one arm to pull down the corner of the blanket that had rolled up. The pain and exhaustion cleared like magic, and all of a sudden I was looking up at the Cheongnyangni tracks stretched across the ceiling.

Wooju must have known that we were not in our usual bed; we tossed and turned together all night.

The next day, when I finally opened my eyes, it was well past ten and Seoyeong was gone. I found a note on her cot that said she'd had to go to an appointment. To think that she had escorted me to the hospital and spent the night on an uncomfortable cot when she had so much to do—I felt my very existence was a burden. I took a little bit of comfort in knowing that I would be able to return this favor someday and felt slightly less sorry. I hadn't told Seoyeong yet, but I had started to sketch out a new play and the opening was more or less finished. It was about a French national Korean adoptee who happens to meet an elderly Korean woman on a trip to Paris—she had secretly sent a daughter born out of wedlock to the city when she was a young woman—and they spend the day together. They are not mother and daughter, but they see mother and daughter in each other as their friendship grows. Or perhaps a bond stronger than friendship. The Korean name of the Korean adoptee in the play is Seoyeong. If the play was ever staged, I hoped to invite Seoyeong, Soyul, and even Eun to France. I wouldn't be able to pay for their travel expenses, but I would be able to give them room and board at my studio apartment. And in the evenings, I wanted to screen Henri's films, which they were interested in seeing. After each movie, we would drink cold beer, reminisce on our time together in Korea, and laugh.

How big would Wooju be then? Would Wooju have made it safely into this world and grown up healthy? Would this be after I told Wooju about the scenes of this summer, the direction of the winds and the color of the leaves and the shapes of clouds in the sky in that moment that Wooju came to be Wooju? All I wanted for Wooju was good health and peace, and it made me sad sometimes to think that some might say that was too much to ask for, given the life I had. Even knowing that no one I knew would ever say anything so cruel, I still couldn't banish the voice, which was suspended like fog in the future I imagined. Not knowing how much time I had remaining often scared me.

The doctor on rounds examined me and said I could rest in the room until my emergency contact came to get me. Anticipating a conflicted reaction from the doctor, I did not tell him that I didn't have a guardian. I was eating the nutritious meal the hospital had provided for lunch when a woman who had just given birth was brought into the room on a gurney. Her husband, parents, and in-laws all followed her, filling up the two-person hospital room with words of congratulations and laughter of relief and joy. As I ate my lunch, I imagined the palm of Henri's hand patting my head. *Nana.* If I looked up slowly, he would have gazed gently down at me with his gray-blue eyes and said my name over and over—*Nana, Nana*—in his gentle voice, as he always had when I was lonely. If only he were alive.

The afternoon went by slowly.

After I checked out of the hospital in the evening, I got on the subway and headed to Cheongnyangni Station instead of Seoyeong's place. Once more, and for the last time in my life, I wanted to see the tracks at Cheongnyangni Station.

# 17

As evening turned to night, all was quiet on the platforms of Cheongnyangni Station.

The crowds and noise on the day we shot the opening scene were as distant as a dream. Apart from platform 5, where a train had pulled in, all the tracks were empty and there were few passersby.

As darkness grew deep, the artificial pools of light around the fluorescent lamps, signs, and vending machines pierced through the dusk. I watched the Mugunghwa train bound for Busan departing from Cheongnyangni Station, got off the bench, and made my way one step at a time to the end of the platform. I closed my eyes. Only when I couldn't see ahead of me was I able to feel Munju walking beside me down to the tracks running parallel to the platform.

Munju hummed as she walked, hands behind her back, like a suspended musical note. A woman like me, or rather, a woman who was exactly me, was here now. The moment I felt her, the imagined sound of her feet treading on the pebbled tracks became the sole occupation of my senses, and the rhythmic footsteps gave me the confidence that I would absolutely be safe walking with my eyes closed. I had stepped outside the screen—I was outside the frame of my life, in Munju's realm.

I felt I could go on and on anywhere with Munju, but my footsteps stopped at the end of the platform. There, I opened my eyes and looked at the track heading into a cave of darkness. It seemed like the tracks would lead to a cold, formless void instead of Daejeon or Busan. Munju headed into the darkness without stopping, almost as if she were marching into battle. As always in my imagination, I did not turn her around.

Munju continued to walk away from me and when she vanished beyond the last point where I could see her, I knew that she had left the tracks for good and that she would never appear in my imagination again. My identity, and the place where I hid my pain for so many years—the tracks no longer defined me. When the tracks ceased to hold power over me, so too did the presumption that my biological mother didn't know any better. A woman in the dark; a lifetime recorded on a few documents and sealed in a black plastic bag; whose whereabouts, even of her grave, were not known and never would be—I found myself no longer able to say I knew anything about her.

A drop of rain fell on my nose, signaling my re-entry into the three-dimensional realm. The cold drop on my skin awakened me to the sound and smell of the rain. More droplets fell. This was nature's clock showing the passage of water to cloud and back to water again. I looked behind me. The flat world of the rectangular screen was no longer there.

When I got back to Seoyeong's, I took a hot shower and was moisturizing my hands and feet when I thought of Yeonhee and her small, wrinkled hands. Did the caretaker notice Yeonhee's long fingernails and carefully clip them? I wondered. No, she wouldn't have, I was certain. Taking care of patients' waste and phlegm and massaging them to prevent bedsores kept the caretakers so busy that they wouldn't notice a small detail like fingernails.

When I had visited Yeonhee three days before, the young nurse repeated what she'd already told me the first time we met: there was no use keeping a patient, unable to receive surgery or treatment, who was waiting for death alone, which was why the hospital would rather move the patient to a home or the hospice wing. But the patient was unconscious and the guardian was just barely showing up to pay the bills, so our hands were tied. I couldn't shake the thought that everyone was waiting for Chu Yeonhee to quietly disappear from this world without causing trouble. It made my blood run cold.

I packed a nail clipper into my purse and counted how many days Yeonhee had been unconscious. She was found in her room two weeks ago, and it was on the same day that I had looked at her account book, so the anniversary of Baek Boksun's death would have come and gone.

"Oh, that's right," I was mumbling to myself as I got some food out of the refrigerator to make dinner, when a few numbers in the margin of her account book floated up like empty bags, rippling the surface of my memory. I dropped everything and rushed out the door. The numbers had to be the phone number of someone who knew where Baek Boksun was buried.

I went down the twenty-seven rain-soaked steps to the first floor to find Bokhee's Kitchen had been padlocked. I supposed the landlord had come after hearing the news and locked the restaurant up. I went around the back. There was a small clearing where the trash was taken out for pickup, and a few windows connected to Yeonhee's room. I stacked some boxes from the pile of recyclables outside Yeonhee's window and climbed into her room without difficulty. The shelf under the window made for a sturdy stepping stone. When I turned on the table lamp, the same amber light spread throughout the room instantly and the familiar sight of small furniture, worn out clothes, and the fan with a broken wing came into view.

Yeonhee's account book still lay open on her bed the way she'd left it. In the margin next to items like rice cake, mung bean powder, pears, and apples was a number she had scrawled down. I keyed it into my phone and pressed the call button. The phone rang about ten times before the call was connected. A middle-aged woman answered, her voice raspy as though she'd been sleeping.

"Baek Boksun . . ." I began cautiously. "Baek Boksun . . . is the grave of someone called Baek Boksun over there?"

"What?" The woman sounded irritated, but she did not hang up. After a bout of crackling sounds, the woman said something that included many words I didn't know. "*Wipae, jae wa siju, yeongga . . .*"

I was going to write them down in the margins of Yeonhee's account book and ask what they meant, but it was impossible to stay on the phone. The noise outside was so loud that I couldn't focus on what the woman was saying. First came the explosive sound of glass breaking, then a shrill voice droning on and on.

---

It was the old woman with the cart.

The old woman had shattered the glass door of Bokhee's Kitchen with something and was now crumpled on the debris cursing at I couldn't tell who. Her grimy brassiere was exposed under the stretched-out collar of her damp cotton T-shirt, and one leg of her floral-print pants had ridden up to her knee. Her calves and arms bore several cuts and scrapes from the broken glass, and blood was oozing out of them.

People stole quick glances at her as they passed by, but it seemed the old woman had already lost any sense of self-consciousness. When I got closer, I was overwhelmed by the stench of alcohol fumes, along with city trash and ripe sweat—the revolting smell was unlike anything I had experienced before.

"It's mine, everything in the restaurant is mine. Who's going around locking my stuff up in there? Whose bright idea was it, huh? Am I right, Third Floor?"

The old woman glared up at me, her pleading, innocent eyes welling up under the unkempt salt-and-pepper hair clinging to her face. The rain began to fall again. The windows of nearby buildings quickly shut, and the alley filled with the rising and falling sound of the rain. The sound reminded me of burning logs.

I grabbed her by the arms and was pulling her to her feet to get her out of the rain when she muttered, "It's all your fault."

"What?"

"You pulled it all out, Third Floor. I forgot it all. It was almost all erased, but you brought it all back. All of it!"

The cold rain must have sobered her up a little. She grew increasingly loud, until the veins were popping out of her neck and she was able to get up on her own. She staggered into the restaurant muttering, "I erased too much. Too many . . . I stopped counting after seven. But . . . but I know. It's scary how well I know. All of it . . . Eleven. I erased eleven."

The old woman did not stop muttering even as she stumbled over to the refrigerator, took out a bottle of soju, drank from the bottle, and wiped her mouth hard on her sleeve. Standing with my back to the broken glass door, I looked over at the old woman. Our eyes met and turned away mid-air.

The old woman was about to tell the story not of Yeonhee or Bokhee, but of herself. I could feel it. Because she had been wanting to tell her story all along. Because she was unable to hide her envy that bordered on resentment when I showed interest in Yeonhee's life story. The old woman was as old as Yeonhee, old enough to yearn for someone to remember the good and bad she had been through, or maybe just the fact that she had been in this world. Bokhee's Kitchen was about to be her stage, and the streetlight filtering in, her spotlight. I was to be her sole audience member in an otherwise empty house.

The old woman began her story.

When she was a young woman working at a club in the old gijichon, she periodically became pregnant, and when pregnant went straight to the public clinic to receive the procedure. For women who worked at the gijichon, the procedure was as a routine as getting tested for STDs. The old woman's life took a turn for the worse after her eleventh procedure. Her pregnancy was successfully terminated, but her uterus was beyond repair. The clinic doctor told her that she would never get pregnant again. She didn't care. She had no intention of bringing another life into this godforsaken world anyway.

The problem came after the procedure. Each time she had sex, she suffered excruciating pain as if her flesh were being torn. She could not work anymore. It was impossible. No one asked for the woman now that she was damaged goods, and she was banished to the back room. The club owner and staff, the regulars and a few soldiers she used to meet like lovers, turned their backs on her in an instant. She had nothing but the debt she owed the club owner—she was surprised to find that the bill included the eleven procedures—and a few tablets of Optalidon, a poor man's lorazepam. She had a feeling then that she would be sold off to a filthier, even more out-of-the-way place.

"So what happened?" I asked coldly. She must not have detected the lack of warmth in my voice. Her expression remained unchanged as she took another swig of soju from the bottle and plopped down in an empty chair. A car passed by just then, bathing the side of her face with bright headlights. For a second in the light, she looked like a young woman.

"I ran away. Escaped. I broke out at dawn and went to Seoul Station to buy a train ticket. But then I realized that I had nowhere to go. I had cut off ties with my parents, my brothers and sisters, and lived for decades in Itaewon. Where on earth could I go? So I drank the rest of the money I had on me, and my legs took me back to Itaewon. I knew I would be finished if the club owner caught me, but I thought I'd rather die. I'd rather die in Itaewon. So I took off my pumps somewhere in the neighborhood and fell asleep using them as a pillow, and she found me on the way home from work. She said she saw me a few times at the clinic. She came over to me first.

"The chummy people who were calling me *unnie* and honey just yesterday tossed me out like garbage. But then there was this woman who took me into her own home, fed me and brought me medicine even though she didn't know me. She said I should hide out at her place in case word got around. That her house was safe. I didn't know what she was giving me, but I sure didn't miss Optalidon anymore. I felt okay for a while.

"Yeah, you're right, Third Floor. I actually know Baek Boksun. She was there when I was there. An eighteen-year-old girl who still had her baby fat, and already huge with child . . . I must have seen her around. She looked familiar, but we had never spoken before. Baek Boksun said she started working at a factory when she was fifteen. But the damn factory kept stealing her wages, so she went looking for work at a temp agency, which landed her in Itaewon."

The old woman said that Baek Boksun was in the final stage of pregnancy then. Took pregnant at work, so she was driven out like the old woman and was being protected at Yeonhee's home.

For one season, the old woman lived as a member of the family that Yeonhee had put together. When Yeonhee went to work, the old woman took care of chores around the house, and looked after Bokhee when Baek Boksun was bedridden after giving birth. She would hold Bokhee, play with her, and wash her. She laughed. The old woman could laugh again thanks to Bokhee. The old woman was Bokhee's third mother and another family member that Bokhee would not remember. But the reason the old woman had to leave Yeonhee's home after just one season was, ironically, because of Bokhee, who'd brought laughter back to her.

Bokhee reminded the old woman of the eleven children who had disappeared without ever seeing the light of this world, and she could not bear it. Torn apart and pulled out with surgery tools, flesh and bones tossed in the garbage and blood washed down the drain. If these children had lived, if they weren't killed, they would have laughed, cried, fussed, and survived any way they could, like Bokhee. The thought brought on pain, the pain of her insides rotting.

One day the old woman left Yeonhee's home without a word and left Itaewon as well. She left without a second thought, so easily that she couldn't believe she wasn't able to do so until that day, and returned after Baek Boksun died and Bokhee was adopted. The old woman and Yeonhee were both in their forties by then. The club owner who'd been after the old woman was fortunately in prison. Yeonhee was an empty shell, going back and forth between the clinic and her house without a spark of life in her eyes. A middle-aged woman growing old alone. Not long after, it was Yeonhee's turn to leave Itaewon. The old woman had seen it coming, and she believed she would never see Yeonhee again. And then Yeonhee suddenly returned after twenty years and opened the restaurant.

"Looking for Baek Boksun's grave? There's no grave. They plowed down the entire hill and built houses and churches on top. Who would have thought to gather her remains when her grave had no tombstone or marker? Yeonhee wasn't here when it happened. There's no urn holding Baek Boksun's ashes somewhere, understand?

"But you know what, Third Floor? I envy Baek Boksun. I envy her so much it drives me crazy. She got Bokhee. She protected her. Bokhee lived. She lived, she's all grown up, and she's looking for her mother's grave now. I'm alone, and

I'll be unceremoniously dumped in some mass grave somewhere. That's how my cursed life will end.

"Tell her. Tell her she missed her. She missed her so much it ate her up inside. She would go so far as to say she would gladly die tomorrow if she could see Bokhee today. Please tell Bokhee."

I only listened. Not allowing any expression to appear on my face, trying not to let any emotion dwell in me.

"And . . . Paju . . . Tell her to go to Paju. There's a temple there called Bogwangsa. Yeonhee put a wipae there for Baek Boksun—a wooden tablet that has the deceased's name and date of death on it. The wipae is considered the person's spirit, so the family has memorial rites."

All the pieces fell into place. The woman I spoke to on the phone in Yeonhee's room was the manager at the temple in Paju. Yeonhee had prepared a small place for Baek Boksun, who could not be protected even in death, to rest her soul. Yeonhee would have gone periodically to see the wipae, and prayed that Baek Boksun's soul would rest in peace and freedom.

I went into the kitchen and found an unopened package of dishcloths in the second drawer under the sink. I soaked a dishcloth with water, took it back to the old woman, and washed the blood off her arms and legs as carefully as I could, and admitted to myself the enormous hostility I was harboring toward her. The hostility was rooted in the fact that she had turned her back on so many lives, but that wasn't all. She'd thought that the eleven lives were better off having disappeared without ever setting foot in this world, rather than going through separation and abandonment—the very same despairing thought I'd had. To understand the old woman was to harbor hostility toward her but at the same time to empathize with her decision. This was a layered hostility, one big and one small.

"Hey, believe it or not," the old woman said in a gentler tone, having no idea of what was going on in my head, "I chose to come to Itaewon to make money by singing and making love. I was not like Baek Boksun. Not at all. I was privileged at one time, you know that? I only slept with guys I wanted to sleep with. You can't guess in your wildest dreams what a big deal that was in Itaewon, Third Floor. All those bastards who thought of me as an animal, a whore, a slut! All of them! Underneath my feet! They were all underneath my feet. All of them. No woman in Korea was freer than I was in those days. Let me tell you! I had the world underneath my feet, and I laughed in the face of everything! But then! But then . . . But now all I have is this body. This body that smells like rot, this body that no one wants to touch. It's a wonder, you know? It's a wonder . . . how I turned old so suddenly. It's a wonder that I can still get lonelier than I am now. It's really something, that I have more days to live. That I have to open my eyes and wake up tomorrow . . ."

The old woman laughed, showing the dark hole of her mouth. She laughed and cried at the same time.

I finished washing her arms and legs. I did not know her name, and I would never know. I would never know her name, but I knew that if I thought of her again after a long time, her younger days would come to mind first, even though I had never seen them firsthand. I would think of her on a night like this, for instance:

The woman stumbles out of a noisy club filled with music and rowdy laughter and leans against the wall. This is before she falls into the grip of alcohol, when her face is not as dark, her teeth not rotted through and her body smells of nothing but perfume, and she has the languorous movements of a cat who knows how to be loved. The blinking neon sign of the club flashes on her thick makeup, and the woman looks down at a yellow flower growing out of a crack in the wall. She bends down and picks it. In the club, men who want to go to bed with her are calling out her name. The woman throws the flower on the ground and smiles with overflowing sadness as she looks back. She does not love any of them. She believes no one can own or control her.

One day in the far future, on a day when a loneliness much more profound than usual overcomes me, my loneliness will be completed with the help of this day from the old woman's life long ago. The loneliness will be projected back and forth between her and me until I can no longer tell them apart. Life passes by in such a flash you can hardly believe it isn't just a dream, and all that settles on the bottom is loneliness and bitterness. . . .

*Sorry, my darling. But sometimes, that's life.*

# 18

A week later, Baek Bokhee arrived in Korea.

Seoyeong, Soyul, and Eun all came to the airport with me to film the scene where I meet Baek Bokhee for the first time. Baek Bokhee had given her consent in an email I had sent her about Seoyeong's film.

At the arrival gate, I spotted Baek Bokhee right away among the people trickling out. I had looked at the recent picture she had sent me by email, but I would have recognized her just based on the baby photo Yeonhee had shown me. I imagined she had her mother's eyes and lips. At first glance, she appeared to be of African descent due to her dark complexion and curly hair, but a closer look revealed her

Asian features. The person who looked "number one" like me . . . When Yeonhee had shown me Bokhee's picture and told me that, I'd thought she was coming from a more emotional place, but I could now see what she had meant. We had different skin color and figures, but if our faces were superimposed, some of the lines on them would naturally match up. I remembered the sudden power outage that night, how my footsteps were drawn to the candlelight, Yeonhee's shadow undulating on the wall and the gentle flavor of the white soft-tofu soup that calmed my stomach.

Baek Bokhee came over to us when I waved, and we hugged each other with a smile. Seoyeong's camera was on, and Soyul and Eun were each holding the boom and the lighting panel. My conversation with her could not have flowed more naturally, partly because we were speaking French and partly because she was very expressive. She looked genuinely surprised when she said she couldn't believe summer in Korea, which she remembered as colder than the North Pole, was hotter than in Brussels, and sounded genuinely disappointed when she said her live-in boyfriend could not join her on this trip because he was busy with work. Having heard about the wipae through email, she said that she hoped to visit the temple in Paju alone the next day after unpacking at the hotel. Of course, there was a place she needed to go before getting to the hotel, and I was to accompany her there.

Bokhee and I sat side by side on the airport express. She called me Munju instead of Nana, and I asked her if she knew the meaning of "Bokhee."

"I know what it means, but I don't know the Chinese characters," Bokhee replied. Eun wrote something in a notepad and passed it to Bokhee (白福禧). Bokhee clapped for joy like a child when Eun told her that this was her name. As she looked at the characters, her face turned serious. She knitted her brow as though she were reminded of something, and she rubbed her face with the palms of her hands. There was no way she did not know that Bokhee was the combination of Boksun's "bok" and Yeonhee's "hee." She must have been picturing what I had pictured once: the young Yeonhee and the girl Boksun looking down at the baby, contemplating her name. One of them would have come up with taking a syllable from each of their names, and the other would have instantly agreed. Baek Bokhee, a name embodying two people's hope of protecting one life.

I told Bokhee that Yeonhee had left Itaewon a few years after Bokhee was adopted, and came back twenty years later to open a restaurant, which she named after her. She smiled and asked for the address of the restaurant, then looked up the location on her phone. I couldn't tell her what the old woman had told me. To tell her about how Boksun and Yeonhee met and how the old woman had lived in their house for one season looking after Bokhee, I would have to reveal Baek Boksun's occupation—and that was absolutely not for me to tell. But Bokhee must have known about Baek Boksun's job. The color of Bokhee's skin and the fact that she lived in Itaewon were irrefutable clues. When she found out what people called her mother, how she was treated and how she had lived, Bokhee's pain would have begun. This was the kind of pain no one could presume to know.

To give Yeonhee and Bokhee space, we stayed out in the hall. I had not been able to bring myself to tell Bokhee that Yeonhee would not last through the summer, but she seemed to understand based on Yeonhee's age and condition that this would be the last time she would see her.

Bokhee came out of Yeonhee's room about an hour later. She seemed tired from the complicated feelings she would have gone through while she was with Yeonhee, but she was her characteristically cheery self when she patted me on the shoulder and said she was okay.

"I'm really okay, Munju. It's Yeonhee who's sick, not me." Her voice, which seemed to originate from the heart rather than the vocal cords, quivered lightly.

Bokhee was staying at a hotel not far from the hospital, so we decided to have dinner together. When we asked Bokhee if there was any Korean food she craved when she was in Belgium, she thought hard and replied, "Jajangmyeon."

Seoyeong, Soyul, and Eun all smiled the same smile at her response. When I asked about the meaning of their smiles, Soyul explained in English for Bokhee that all Koreans had at least one memory of jajangmyeon, and it was nice and surprising to see that dish was what she missed the most. Come to think of it, at train conductor Jung Woosik's house and even at the orphanage, jajangmyeon was what we had on special occasions.

"It's a shame that Baek Boksun's grave is gone." I carefully brought up the topic with Bokhee as we slowly made our way to the jajangmyeon restaurant. It had been weighing heavily on me.

"The remains in a grave are just minerals. Knowing that Mother's soul is resting in the wipae in the light and breeze, not entombed in a dark, stuffy coffin, is actually a relief."

Bokhee smiled faintly, and I smiled with her in spite of myself, but I could not banish the thought that Yeonhee may not have so much as a wipae to be remembered by after she was gone. There seemed little chance that someone would keep her wipae in a temple and visit her every year on the anniversary of her death. The old woman did not have the money for it, and Bokhee and I were only in the country temporarily and unable to take responsibility, nor did we owe it to Yeonhee. How often would I think of Yeonhee once I returned? Hardly ever, most likely. Even though I knew that all beings are as alone as a bare-bottomed child when the end came, it felt as if the ground under me were suddenly giving out.

After dinner, I accompanied Bokhee to the hotel, located near the City Hall. On our walk, I could feel the inquisitive eyes of a few passersby. The thoughtless, wounding stares showed xenophobic curiosity. Bokhee stepped aside against the walls often, exhausted by the staring.

Once she'd checked in at the hotel, I watched as Bokhee headed toward the elevators with her suitcase. She looked over her shoulder several times, always with the same exhausted look. She was born Baek Bokhee and living as Stefanie, a woman who looked "number one" like me. Our resemblance perhaps did not stop at our eyes or the shape of our mouths. In certain scenes in our lives we would have stood in the same stance, wearing the same look, thinking the same thoughts as we contemplated the glass wall that stood between us and the rest of the world. Both of us people with folds and tears in our lives that were achingly similar, beyond facial features.

# 19

Two days after Bokhee came to Korea, Mungyeong got in touch with me asking to meet.

When I arrived at the coffee shop where we had agreed to meet, I couldn't seem to stop pacing around the table. It was because of the woman Mungyeong had agreed to bring. Behind the espresso bar, Seoyeong was discussing camera angles with Soyul and Eun. They were setting up at a nearby table when I heard the jingle of the door chime behind me.

Despite my wish to see her as soon as possible, I moved each muscle incredibly slowly to turn around and look at the door. Mungyeong was guiding her slowly toward me. The woman who had clicked her tongue every time our eyes met but washed me clean every night and patted me on the tummy until I fell asleep; the woman who did not appreciate the sight of me sitting at the table but made snacks from a grain called susu every time it rained and filled the house with the scent of wet wood.

"Aga . . ."

She came toward me and called me. Instantly, a volume dial somewhere on the border between memory and oblivion was turned up, and a few scenes from the past rang out "*aga*" like bells. On days when she was feeling good, and on days when she looked sad after drinking, she called me *aga* instead of Munju, and her voice was generally warm. Her words from those days were coming back to me.

*Aga, you have to eat your veggies to grow tall. Aga, did you have a bad dream too last night? Aga, be well. No matter what, be well.*

"Oh, oh my goodness. Oh my goodness, is that really you, aga? Is that really you?" she asked over and over as she lifted one hand and stroked my face with it. Her hand was raw-boned. Not just her hands, but her entire body was so small and thin that it confused me. In my memory, she had a robust figure, and the silhouette of her stomach and waist was round, her posture straight, and her steps quick and even when she was carrying a heavy load on her head or moving things. While I was living in France as Henri and Lisa's daughter, growing up to be an actor and playwright, she had turned into a wizened old woman with her upper body strangely curved in. If she had indeed aged much more rapidly than the average human being, I supposed it was due to time eating away at her after she lost her son.

"How . . . have you been?" she asked. "Woosik is no longer with us. You can't see him. Woosik is gone."

When I placed my hand on hers and asked after her, she looked at me with teary eyes but gave a strange reply. I managed to remember Mungyeong telling me that she was hard of hearing. "Gone, gone," she said repeatedly but kept her hand pressed against my cheek.

Only after she had calmed down were the three of us able to sit. Mungyeong sat next to her and told me that her grandmother unfortunately did not know which Chinese characters were used in "Munju." Seoyeong's camera light went on, and Soyul and Eun went to their places to adjust position and angle.

"I just figured you were Munju because Woosik called you Munju," she said, having understood what Mungyeong was saying right away. *It doesn't matter,* I thought to myself. I didn't care if Munju meant door pillars or dust, or even some code the train conductor Jung Woosik had picked out of a phone book. It didn't matter to me anymore, I told Mungyeong and her grandmother truthfully. The instant shift inside the heart of the train conductor Jung Woosik when he named the child he found on the tracks Munju, or how he must have felt when he heard a similar name years later—maybe these were the things I wanted to know, not the meaning of the name Munju. I wanted to know about the stories outside the screen that no one could know now.

"I didn't think to ask what it meant back then. If I had known how important it would be to you . . . I'm sorry, aga," she said.

I told her there was nothing to be sorry about and smiled as brightly as I could, but she hung her head in a way I had never seen her do all those years ago, and kept repeating that it was her fault.

"By the way, Grandma says Dad found you in the waiting area at the Cheongnyangni Station," Mungyeong said, changing the subject.

Mungyeong's tone suggested she did not know the grave significance of what she had just shared, but a part of my heart had already crumbled inside. When I squeezed Mungyeong's hand hard and told her I wanted to hear more about the waiting area, she picked up on my urgency and hurriedly said into her grandmother's ear, "Munju-unnie was wearing a red dress, right? And that caught Dad's eye? Is that what you told me, Grandma?"

She nodded slowly.

Train conductor Jung Woosik had first found me in the waiting area of the station, not on the tracks. A girl in a red dress wandering without a guardian in a train station waiting room would have stood out. Crossing the waiting area to get to work as always, he would have watched me closely and thought about the red dress as he boarded the control car. Mungyeong explained that in those days the control room was full of engine exhaust and high-decibel noises, a difficult place to make quick, rational decisions. She said that he was perhaps able to pull the brakes the moment he saw the small red ball on the tracks because he had already seen her in the waiting room. A small, fragile creature cloaked in a bold color as if to say, *See me* . . .

Seoyeong's speculation that I wasn't abandoned on the tracks had turned from possibility to reality. The wounds I had built on the tracks no longer held up, and I had to redefine my biological mother. Pardoned by her past and her name cleared at last, she was a person who did not intend for me to get injured or killed. . . .

"I want to know your name," I said, looking in her direction.

Mungyeong relayed my question to her once again, and with a look in her eyes that was different from before, she slowly answered, "Suja. I'm Park Suja. My father gave me that name. Goodness, it's been so long since I told anyone my name."

Park Suja smiled brightly for the first time since she came into the coffee shop. Mungyeong explained that many women of her grandmother's generation had *ja* in their names, a custom that remained from the Japanese occupation. Park Suja took my right hand, pulled it close to her, and began to slowly write something in my palm. 秀. *Su*. Mungyeong said it meant "exceptional beauty." Park Suja wrote two more Chinese characters in my hand, which Mungyeong said were *woo* and *sik*. I clenched my hand hard, as if to say that I would not let the letters evaporate, that I would keep the touch and warmth of her hand in my palm for always. Seeing someone you know you'll never see again—I could understand the kind of loneliness Bokhee would have experienced in Yeonhee's hospital room.

That afternoon, I got in Mungyeong's car with Park Suja to visit Yeongwol, Park Suja's hometown and the place where Jung Woosik's ashes were laid to rest.

Seoyeong planned to drive Soyul and Eun down in a separate car she'd borrowed from Eun's family to continue filming in Yeongwol.

After a three-hour drive, we arrived at the columbarium. Park Suja walked ahead of Mungyeong, leading us up a wooded path to a light-gray four-story building. Standing before Jung Woosik's drawer-sized unit by the second-floor window, I looked at the neat arrangement of vase, cross, many picture frames, and a white urn containing his ashes. Park Suja opened the glass door of the unit, pulled out a picture frame, wiped it several times with her hand, and passed it to me. In the frame was the face of Jung Woosik when he was old, one I had never seen. I closed my eyes. The sugary taste of the biscuit, his firm bones when he carried me on his back, and the young voice that called me Munju . . . Stretched out beyond these senses like a path of fresh snow was the life of a man who married, had children, suffered an illness, and died. The man in the picture was the sum of the senses left in me and the scenes I never saw.

I hugged the frame to my chest and stood for a while. For a moment, all the light around me went out.

Mungyeong was going to stay with her grandmother for the night, and I was to get a ride with Seoyeong.

Before we parted, Mungyeong said, "I think Dad liked that the character *mun* had the meaning of 'pattern.' I think that's why he put it in your name. So if *mun* means pattern, then what's *ju*? I think he had wooju—the universe—in mind."

"Wooju?" I had to ask, smiling.

Mungyeong, who had no way of knowing what a great coincidence "pattern of the universe" was for me, said rather soberly, "Mungyeong and Munju. 'Pattern of sunlight' and 'pattern of the universe.' If we had grown up together, people would have thought that they were the perfect names for sisters."

Come to think of it, "Munju" and "Wooju" shared one character. It wouldn't be an exaggeration to say that "Wooju" and "Mungyeong" were closely connected too, since I had thought of the name under the light filtering through the trees. If Mungyeong's assumption were wrong, I still wanted to believe it, and I fully believed it by the time we stepped out of the columbarium.

It was time for us to part.

As we said our final goodbyes, Park Suja stroked my face with her bony hands as she had at the coffee shop and bid me and my child good health. *Be well, no matter what.* It sounded like her way of telling me to survive and live on. I wanted to say something in response—*I will. Thank you.*—but in the end I couldn't say the words.

Before Park Suja got into the car with Mungyeong's help, she turned around and looked at me. She wasn't looking at me, but at a light inside of me that only she recognized. The light had been turned on and guarded by her son, and so she had the right to look at this living person. As I watched Mungyeong's car drive off, I realized that I had seen Park Suja and Lisa in Yeonhee just as Yeonhee had searched for Bokhee in me. If the light in me made its way into Yeonhee's heart, that was thanks to Park Suja and Mungyeong as well.

On the highway back up to Seoul that evening, I received an email from Baek Bokhee on my phone. The email began with an apology for her abrupt departure due to a problem at her company where she worked as an accountant.

—

*I'm so sorry to say I had to move my flight up to tonight.*

*But I can say without a moment's hesitation that the last three days, visiting the temple in Paju and seeing Yeonhee at the hospital, were the most fulfilling of my life. These three days have forever changed my life from here on out. I stopped by Bokhee's Kitchen yesterday as well. I went up to the third floor where you told me you were staying to say hello, but you weren't there. But I have to tell you, I laughed so hard at the Bokhee's Kitchen sign.*

*To tell you the truth, going back to that neighborhood took some courage on my part. I don't know if you can imagine what a child who looked like me would have gone through in 1980s Korea.*

*I always knew that I looked different, but I didn't know I could be discriminated against, even abused for it, until I started school. My schoolmates never called me by my name. I was called by so many nicknames, and kids made up new ones every day. Most of them were awful names that were sexual and insulting. Where did children who were not even ten years old hear such words? Once I started school, not a day went by when I did not get hurt, in body or feelings. When I got home, I sat in a dark room without turning on the lights, neither eating nor sleeping, waiting for Yeonhee to come back from work.*

*In retrospect, hatred was the only thing that got me through those days. It wasn't the unjust world or the parents who dragged me into it that I hated, but myself, for being born. During that time, Yeonhee was not just a guardian but a friend, a healer, and the only person on earth who shared a life with me. Yeonhee would come home from work at the clinic and clean or treat the new cuts and bruises of the day and hug me. This was an important daily ritual for me and Yeonhee. "This will pass," she would say. "There's nothing in life that doesn't pass with time," Yeonhee would say, and I would be able to breathe again. Yeonhee would have grown weary as we went through this process again and again. I am aware. I was aware then, too, but chose to ignore it. My pain was greater than Yeonhee's, or so it seemed, so I believed it was her duty to comfort me.*

*The moment I saw Yeonhee lying unconscious on the hospital bed, I remembered a scene I had long forgotten: in the middle of winter, Yeonhee was watching me as I waddled home in my urine-soaked frozen pants. I couldn't use the bathroom at school because kids did and said far more abusive things in the bathroom than in the classroom. I ended up wetting my pants that day, sat in my wet pants until school was over, then ran into Yeonhee on the way home. I had never seen Yeonhee so angry. She pulled and shoved me very hard as she dragged me home, peeled off my clothes, and washed me up, but I was strangely not scared. On the contrary, I felt sad and sorry for Yeonhee. Because she was crying the whole time.*

*That must have been the day Yeonhee decided to put me up for adoption. I said in my previous letter that I couldn't understand why Yeonhee chose to put me up for adoption, but perhaps I didn't understand because I didn't want to understand. At the hospital, when I thought back to that scene, I finally felt the courage or desire to hug Yeonhee the way she'd hugged me. The moment I hugged Yeonhee, I could feel that the person I was holding was both Yeonhee and, at the same time, the little girl I once was.*

*I am grateful to you for giving me this opportunity. I cannot thank you enough and I truly respect you, but in order for us to meet again, I will have to get to a place where I am so happy that reflecting on the past does not bring me pain. You may have guessed it, but I am getting time off from work to receive surgery. When the surgery is over, a long, long treatment of chemotherapy will begin. Even if the process casts a grim shadow on my life, I am certain that I will be a happier person going forward. I will survive, and I will be as happy as a person can hope to be.*

*I hope the day will come, Munju. Years from now, I will call you first, ask you how you are, and suggest we meet immediately to eat and drink together.*

*Until that day comes, I wish you and your child the best of health.*

*Sincerely,*
*Baek Bokhee*

# 20

Yeonhee died.

Four days after Baek Bokhee returned to Belgium, I stopped by the hospital in the morning. I had emptied Yeonhee's urine bag and was massaging her arms and legs when I felt a shudder at my fingertips. I could tell that this was different from her usual movements. The trembling seemed to pass through not just Yeonhee's body, but time itself. Adrift in the sea of time without beginning or end, quivers transmitted from the body of a human being hopelessly capsizing . . .

I reflexively took a few steps back and gazed numbly into Yeonhee's face for a while. She had the same uninhibited face that made it look like she was sleeping, but there was an energy flowing around her that I had never felt before. It was a cool energy. Cool yet peaceful. Was Yeonhee ready to leave but waiting for someone? Perhaps she had been preparing for this moment since the day Baek Bokhee came to see her.

I sat back down by Yeonhee's side and held her hand, bracing myself for the enormous sadness that would soon come over me. Her unsettlingly cold hands broke my heart. As I'd done with Henri long ago, I rubbed my face again and again in Yeonhee's palm like a kitten. I closed my eyes. Leaving her depleted body, Yeonhee would arrive at the shapeless darkness to begin an everlasting journey as a pinch of matter or energy, or a seed, or a whirl of smoke. Back to what she was before she came into this world, before she was even a cell, billions of years of evolution ago.

"Rest in peace," I said.

*You worked so hard to go on living . . . To survive . . . Goodbye, Yeonhee.*

*Goodbye . . .*

*Goodbye . . .*

"Goodbye, goodbye," I whispered and buried my face in her chest.

Yeonhee's hand twitched as if to say goodbye one last time. I slowly opened my eyes. I saw a few patients, guardians, and caretakers from the same floor huddled by the door. The nurses came to see what was going on, and soon returned with doctors. Yeonhee's doctor soberly checked her pulse and pupils and listened to her chest. When he called time of death, the nurse recorded it in her chart, and the young doctors who appeared to be interns collected the transparent and opaque tubes from her body. When the medical staff had gone, two well-built men came into the room, covered Yeonhee's body with a white gown, moved her onto a gurney, and took her to the morgue.

Everything had happened so quickly that it didn't feel real. I sat on Yeonhee's bed looking out the window as though I were waiting for someone. This hospital room after Yeonhee had gone—was it happening on- or off-screen? I could not tell. The only thing I knew for certain was this: Yeonhee did not exist in this room anymore.

Yeonhee died.

After living through acts and scenes I didn't dare pretend to know, Yeonhee had died, and it signified the end of one universe called Chu Yeonhee.

I could clearly make out the dust rising and falling outside the hospital room window each time the wind blew. Nurses and doctors strode by, patients in threes and fours were out on a walk or gathered for a chat, and children ran about, weaving through the adults. The scenery was alive. Proof of life such as voices, laughter, and footsteps made small whirlwinds here and there with clouds of dust. The bedsheets still held the warmth and scent of Yeonhee's body, but her existence had just now turned into an absence, and it could never, ever be reversed. It seemed the world outside the window would never reconcile to this fact. The only proof of Yeonhee that remained now was the death certificate signed by the doctor, the authentication of death with the municipal government stamp on it, the termination forms for various personal accounts, the inheritance certification documents, the insurance payment receipt for the beneficiary, the receipt for the hospital bill that would be paid off with the insurance payment, and the key deposit from Bokhee's Kitchen. Documents were all that remained—pieces of paper that certified one life had ended.

Time passed.

Around noon, the young nurse who had asked me to check on Yeonhee's breathing came by. Her voice was filled with sorrow as she sat down next to me and said she had heard that Yeonhee had passed. I wasn't able to accept her death yet, so in some way the nurse was the first mourner to come by and grieve Yeonhee's death. The nurse said that the hospital got in touch with Yeonhee's younger sister. She told me that the family wished to forgo the funeral and move straight to the cremation, then scatter the ashes in the mountains or fields rather than keep them in an urn in a columbarium. Yeonhee would be leaving no small vessel in this world for her soul; instead she would completely sever all ties as she departed. I felt more keenly than I ever had that Yeonhee was completely alone and a much lonelier person than I could have imagined.

The young nurse tried a few times to say something, held back until our eyes met, and finally let me know that there was a patient waiting to take this room. The nurse's words translated as, *New deaths are waiting outside the door.* Perhaps the hospital room was neither on-screen nor off, but just a waiting room between life and death. I got off the bed. As most people had begun to do recently, the nurse wished me a healthy delivery and left.

Yeonhee died.

I gathered the towels and underwear to throw out, gave the leftover diapers and wet tissues to the shared caretaker, and had nothing left to do. Before I left the room, I looked down at the bed that would soon be occupied by someone else. Sunlight that came from eternity and was heading to eternity had formed a pool around the bed. I remembered vowing to be a witness to Yeonhee's death. I had done my duty by bearing witness to her death just now, so all that remained was to announce it to the world and to grieve together.

*Giving Yeonhee a proper send-off, that is how I will welcome your arrival . . .*

—

When I left the hospital, I stopped by the supermarket on the way to Seoyeong's apartment. I brought beef, salmon, spaghetti, onions, mushrooms and carrots, cream sauce and basil. I arrived at Bokhee's Kitchen by cab to find the glass door that the old woman had broken still shattered.

Stepping on broken glass, I went into the kitchen and began preparing the beef and salmon and washing the vegetables.

*Who's to say?*

*As far as Baek Bokhee is concerned, I really don't know what's best,* I thought and thought as I prepared the ingredients. I wanted to tell myself that it was wrong of me to not tell Baek Bokhee about Yeonhee's death, but I had to admit that I didn't know for sure if telling her was the right thing to do. Like Bokhee said, she would survive, and after a long time we would meet in some city in France or Belgium and talk about Yeonhee's death. On that day, I would tell her slowly when and how Yeonhee had passed away, what the hospital room looked like in that moment, and the last words I said to her. As Bokhee left Korea, she thought that the small space where we would sit together in some distant future was the final respect she would pay to her past, and I understood that. Because I understood it, I was quite unsure about calling her. By the time I was done preparing the ingredients, I had made up my mind not to call Baek Bokhee.

I wanted to believe that the reprieve we received by delaying the truth was also a part of life.

The dinner slowly fell into place. The beef stew, salmon steak, and spaghetti with cream sauce were laid out on the table when the invited guests poured into Bokhee's Kitchen. Seoyeong and Soyul brought chrysanthemums, and Eun brought a cocoon-shaped paper lantern. When I asked about the lantern, he said it was a jodeung—mourner's light—and explained that it was a sign that someone had passed, and that it had to remain lit all throughout the funeral process.

While Eun took a chair to the entrance and put up the lantern, I gazed up at the entrancing light. The clerk from Children's Services appeared with a bottle of cheongju liquor right after the lantern went up.

The meal began. We'd put out a plate even at the empty seats and the guests glanced at them often, as though someone were there, throughout the leisurely meal with wine and cheongju. When it became dark outside, the yellow glow of the lantern spilled into the restaurant and gently shined upon our quiet meal. The light seemed not a sign of death, but a thin film of protection guarding the boundary of life.

After dinner, the guests kept their places at the table where Yeonhee was the person of the hour. Soyul made me warm tea, the clerk brought back a watermelon from a nearby store and cut it into wedges, and Seoyeong and Eun got into a heated debate about recent film releases. I liked the bustle. I sat with my chin propped up and smiled quietly as I listened to their animated discussion.

When the night grew deep, the old woman appeared with her cart as always. She was the last mourner I'd been waiting for. Instead of coming into the restaurant, she stood up as straight as I had ever seen her and looked up at the mourner's light for a long time. The yellow particles cast uneven light and shadows over her face and body, then flowed down into a large pool on the ground.

"There's a blue suit in her closet. It's wrapped in plastic. And the black pumps in the back of the shoe closet. And the pink umbrella. Bring me all of those," the old woman said evenly without taking her eyes off the yellow lantern.

I went inside Yeonhee's room and found the clothing the old woman had asked for. It was a two-piece suit with the sleeves and hems perfectly untouched as if it had never been worn. When I returned to the old woman with the pumps and umbrella as well, she took it all to the back of the building. I quietly followed her. In the yard, she put all the items on the ground, lit up a bundle of paper from the cart, and slipped it into the blue suit. The suit, shoes, and umbrella Yeonhee had prepared for the day she would meet Baek Bokhee again slowly caught fire. The old woman pulled out a few bills from her pocket and threw them on the flames. She said it was money for the journey to the next world.

Mourners had come out of the restaurant and were standing beside me. Seoyeong and Soyul each threw a bill in the fire as well, and the clerk threw in a few of the returned letters that Yeonhee hadn't gotten around to picking up. Among the letters was the first one Baek Bokhee had sent to Yeonhee in ten years. The old woman took off her shirt and pants and threw them in the fire as well, and I took off my cardigan and wrapped it around the old woman who was now in her underwear. The clothes, money, and letters burned quickly. The crackling fibres and paper sounded like Yeonhee's footsteps as she journeyed to the netherworld, and the rising smoke seemed like her soul.

"Go on," the old woman whispered as she sat close to the fire. "Everything that happened here, put it behind you and go . . . Go on . . . And when you get there . . . don't forget . . . Don't forget to call me too."

It was the old woman's last goodbye. She sat by the fire for a long time after that. The glow of the flames flickered on her cheeks and slowly died out. Until the fire went out completely and the smoke dispersed, until the clothes burned to nothing and the ashes scattered into the air, I stood behind the old woman with the rest of the mourners and this picture came to mind: Yeonhee gently floating by Wooju in the darkness, neither recognizing the other. Wooju was traveling beyond time in the evolutionary process of coming into this world, while Yeonhee was traveling the same distance out of this world as her body fell away.

Chu Yeonhee. A person who was happy because she had someone to miss. I would remember this name until the day I died. Remembering this name, along with raising Wooju, would be the respect I would pay to this life.

Yeonhee died.

Yeonhee returned to darkness.

# 21

The first Friday of September was the twenty-second week since Wooju came to me, and one week after Yeonhee had passed away. It was also the day I was leaving Korea.

The final scene of the film was to be shot at the airport, so Soyul and Eun planned to pick up the equipment and come straight to the departure terminal to meet us, and Seoyeong volunteered to pick me up since I had a lot to carry. I was packing before Seoyeong arrived when I heard unusual noises coming from downstairs. I walked down the steps and saw two men moving the tables, chairs, and kitchenware in Bokhee's Kitchen. The sign had already been taken down, and the possessions in Yeonhee's room seemed to have been cleared out as well. All I could do was stand back and bear witness to Bokhee's Kitchen emptying out.

The men loaded the truck with salvageable items to sell, tossed the rest, and installed a blue metal shutter at the door. The landlord must have decided to board up the place until there was a new tenant. The shutter came down with a clank, like curtains at the end of a show. Lastly, the men took down the paper lantern, threw it on the ground, and left in their truck.

When the truck disappeared from view, I picked up the paper lantern and hung it back up. As long as there were people who remembered Yeonhee, we were in mourning, and if we were in mourning, the symbol of that mourning had to stay up. Like a small, yellow bird waking up from its slumber, a golden halo appeared when I switched it on, but the light was dim and the battery must have been wearing down.

I went around to the back of the restaurant. Most of the objects in Yeonhee's room had been thrown out. The fabric closet and dresser drawers were all open, revealing the clothes, socks, and medication inside. The pillow and comforter, bearing footprints, were tossed aside next to the dresser, and the fan with the broken wing and a drying rack warped out of shape were lying on the ground. A large paper box containing shoes, an umbrella, a mirror, and other items caught my eye. I looked inside the box and also saw makeup bottles, towels, combs, and the table lamp. The restaurant sign, with a corner dented, was wedged behind the box. It looked like the headstone of an unmarked grave. In fact, there was no headstone more fitting for Chu Yeonhee than the store sign. She was able to live the last ten years of her life waiting for Baek Bokhee in Bokhee's Kitchen, so the name Bokhee was a fitting epitaph for Yeonhee's life.

I zipped up the closet door and closed the drawers, then dusted the pillow and comforter and folded them neatly. I picked up the fan and drying rack and placed them neatly against the wall, and tidied up the inside of the paper box. I went over to the store sign last and took my time wiping every inch of it with my sleeve, as though putting up a clean sign would mean no one would be able to intrude on Yeonhee's kingdom, as if the sign would protect all her discarded possessions. . . . I placed the sign in the middle of the yard. At the very least, until the trash collectors came by, the sign would prove that this was Yeonhee's territory.

I got up and walked out.

Eyes closed, feeling the breeze on the back of my hand, I walked as slowly as possible. With each step, the world behind me gradually came apart, and my body floated up a little at a time. I felt as though I were walking on air. The place we belonged to before we came into this world, the very same place where the soul goes when it loses its body—maybe that shapeless darkness was the heart of life. I thought

I'd been walking for some time, but I didn't make it far. When I turned around, the world had become colorless. In this colorless world, only the paper lantern shined its yellow light.

In that moment, I felt another stir inside.

Wooju had come one step closer to the world Yeonhee had lived in.

Between Yeonhee and Wooju, on the fulcrum balancing the two worlds, I was standing.

I embraced the wind with my chest. I felt warmth in the gentle breeze that came into my arms. I knew, of course, whose warmth it was.

*It's you,* I whispered.

*Wooju.*

"Wooju," I whispered once more.

# 22

In Montpellier, each day that passes is divided perfectly in two. Mornings are spent writing a new play about a protagonist named Seoyeong, and in the afternoon I do chores that have been put off or read books until Lisa comes home from work and we have dinner and tea together. The mornings and afternoons are not two separate parts but seamlessly connected as one, a fact I am reminded of by the sound of Wooju crying, fussing, whimpering, and the labor it requires. As you know, it's an awfully exhausting, tedious labor. I sometimes despair to think that only surrendering my whole life to it will bring an end to this labor.

Sometimes I watch a movie.

It's the rough cut I received a month ago, one that begins on the tracks of Cheongnyangni Station, then moves to Itaewon and Incheon, Ahyeon and Hapjeong and Yeongwol, and ends at Incheon International Airport. With a protagonist who is Jung Munju and Esther Pak and Nana, featuring Sister Gemma, Jung Mungyeong and Park Suja, and Baek Bokhee . . . I've watched it dozens of times already but it comes across as new each time, perhaps because I am picturing the expressions and gestures of Seoyeong, Soyul, and Eun, who are changing and moving outside the camera frame. And because I remember the summer I spent in Korea and the people I met over the course of that summer.

Today would have gone by just like any other day if I hadn't fallen asleep while watching the film. I dreamt that I was walking through an endless, empty field. I could feel the fresh energy of life every time blades of grass grazed my calves. Night fell before long and an enormous moon sailed down and touched the horizon. The night sky opened up into a glorious, vast universe. The scenery, color, and texture were so vivid that it was as if I were still holding a piece of that field when I woke up.

I went straight to my desk where my laptop is and started this letter to you in a fresh document. Come to think of it, this is my very first letter to you. Perhaps more of a confession than a letter.

You might have guessed, but yes, it's about Wooju.

As I walked along a park trail in Paris last June, I have to admit I was thinking about whether to keep Wooju or not. I thought that each side had to be given equal consideration, and I did my best to weigh the outcomes.

I thought that neither decision was selfish. I thought that using Wooju to alleviate my loneliness and anxiety and flaunting my rich, fulfilling motherhood would be more selfish than not having the child. I was also afraid of Wooju growing up to be the kind of person who becomes accustomed to despair after repeated failures, and ends up the kind of empty person who doesn't try anything anymore. The kind of person who cannot experience the world with their own senses, who cannot see the wrong in having more and living less within the societal constructs, an uncaring bystander no matter what happens to others, a living ghost—if Wooju grew up to be this way, how would I relate to them? But the real fear was this: Wooju taking after me—the most lonely, weak version of myself. I thought of my college years, when I used to think that wasting life and dying lonely was much less dignified than vanishing without being born at all. This was also a period in my life when I focused all my energy on hating the person who recklessly gave me life only to abandon me.

But on that day in June, I chose to have Wooju despite my fears.

Because I am the proof.

Born, rescued, protected, adopted as someone's daughter. Working as actor and playwright, and now Wooju's family. I am the proof of living life. Life that includes even the part of me that used to think I should have been given up before I was born, who is still pulled under by these thoughts from time to time.

Mother, can you hear me?

I'm alive.

I don't know what name you called me by, but there must have been a time when I was your everything.

Please remember that.

Remember that I am alive, here, like this, with so many stories to tell you. Wanting to call you Mother.

It is a request that is separate from forgiving and understanding you.

I wish you peace.

This is my sincere wish for you, forever unchanging.

## About the Author

CHO HAEJIN was born in Seoul, South Korea, in 1976. After earning a master's degree in Korean literature, she began her writing career in 2004 with the literary magazine *Munye Joongang*. Since then, her work has been recognized as testament to the existence and lives of those on the margins of Korean society and those forgotten by history, and has won several prominent literary awards in Korea, including the Shin Dong-yup Literary Award, Young Writer's Award, Lee Hyo-seok Literary Award, Hyungpyeong Literary Award, and Dong-in Literary Award. *Simple Heart* was the winner of both the Daesan Literary Award, a leading literary award in Korea, and the Kim Man-jung Literary Award, and has been published in eight countries. Her other novels include *I Met Loh Kiwan,* which was adapted to film under the title *My Name Is Loh Kiwan* and released on Netflix in 2024.

## About the Translator

JAMIE CHANG is an award-winning literary translator. Her translation of *Kim Jiyoung, Born 1982* was longlisted for the 2020 National Book Awards in Translated Literature. She is the recipient of the Daesan Foundation Translation Grant and a three-time recipient of the Literature Translation Institute of Korea Grant. She lives in Nova Scotia, Canada.